the
delicious torment

Also by Alison Tyler

A Is for Amour
Afternoon Delight
B Is for Bondage
Best Bondage Erotica
Best Bondage Erotica, Volume 2
The Big Book of Bondage
C Is for Coeds
Caught Looking (with Rachel Kramer Bussel)
D Is for Dress-Up
Dark Secret Love
Down and Dirty
E Is for Exotic
Exposed
F Is for Fetish
Frenzy
G Is for Games
Got a Minute?
H Is for Hardcore
The Happy Birthday Book of Erotica
Heat Wave
Hide and Seek (with Rachel Kramer Bussel)
Hurts So Good
I Is for Indecent
J Is for Jealousy
K Is for Kinky
L Is for Leather
Love at First Sting
Luscious
The Merry XXXmas Book of Erotica
Morning, Noon and Night
Naughty or Nice
Never Have the Same Sex Twice
Open for Business
Playing with Fire
Red Hot Erotica
Slave to Love
Sudden Sex
Three-Way

the delicious torment

a story of submission

by ALISON TYLER

CLEiS
PRESS

Published in the United States by Cleis Press, Inc., 2246 Sixth Street, Berkeley, California 94710.

Printed in the United States.
Cover design: Scott Idleman/Blink
Cover photograph: Arman Zhenikeyev/Getty Images
Text design: Frank Wiedemann

First Edition.
10 9 8 7 6 5 4 3 2 1

Trade paper ISBN: 978-1-62778-007-0
E-book ISBN: 978-1-62778-020-9

Introduction

We're on Sunset. Way up in the sky in a penthouse apartment overlooking Los Angeles. It's not today. Or yesterday. But, as my best friend says, "back in the day." I'm ensconced in an S/M relationship that makes everything I've done before turn a whiter shade of pale.

There's truth here. *And* fiction. Reality and fantasy. The lines blur at the edges. The seams fray. The satin strands begin to unravel. But not the bindings. Those leather bindings remain hard and fast, until they're met with the right key.

This is a novel with me at the center. That is, my heroine is based on me. I've sketched her with broad strokes, but at our core we are the same. She's gotten herself entwined with an older man—nothing new there. But now she has to learn how to maneuver a 24/7 relationship. (What one isn't? Aren't all relationships around the clock?)

Of course, with every love affair—whether involving corsets, crops, and kink or not—there are twists and turns. Boundaries to overcome. Safewords to spill. I'm inviting you into the inner sanctum. A place founded in memory and woven with fantasy. My eyes are wide open, ready to experience the seductive, erotic journey all over again.

Take this ride with me.

Go on. Take the ride.

XXX,
Alison

My cast of characters—for those keeping score:

Brock, my first
Byron, my ex
Jack, my current
Alex, his right-hand man

Prologue

I believe you can fall in love six times before breakfast—that is, if you're looking. If you have an aura of willingness, of curiosity, then others will come find you. Jack understood this intimately, and he worked hard to keep my focus on him. But he needn't have worried. At heart, I'm an extremely monogamous person. I wanted to please Byron. Trust me, I did. Yes, I relished the animosity of our breakup, but only because it was so long coming. For years, I did my best to be exactly the type of girl he wanted. I'm sweet by nature, with a dark edge that rarely comes out. I was always more comfortable being left than leaving.

Yet Jack worried. I could tell. He demanded my constant declarations of submission to him. He wanted me to say, "I'm yours."

I wanted him to say something entirely different, but I bided my time.

Jack and I were both high-strung on desire. On the sofa, we sat with limbs entwined. At dinner, we bent close together, feet touching under the table. We fucked everywhere. *Everywhere.* In his car. In his office. On the beach. In Mann's Chinese Theater. Outside of Griffith Observatory.

I was his. He had to know that. But first he made me prove myself to him—through pain, and shame, and utter humiliation.

And, trust me, shame can be more painful than pain itself.

Chapter One:
Love Me Two Times

I came in the night.

This had happened to me before, but not often. Wet dreams are more rare for women, I think, than for men. But I came. Hard. Picturing Jack using a cane on me, my body bent, knees under my stomach, ass up to receive each blow. The climax was exquisite, and I was covered with a thin sheen of sweat when Jack shook me awake.

"What was that?"

I responded with a sound between a moan and a sigh, lost in my dream.

"Sam, what the fuck was that?"

By now I was slightly more awake, and chilled. Did Jack know what had happened? Could he guess? Normally, a sleep-induced climax might not have been a big deal. But Jack had been working with me, training me to come when he wanted me to come. He'd put me on restriction—this was my second day with no climax—second of a threatened five. That's how greedy I am for pleasure. I couldn't turn off my desires.

My body, subconsciously, had disobeyed him.

Even through the dream haze, some part of me wanted to be insolent. *Earthquake*, I thought to say. But self-preservation kicked in. Instead, pretending to be drowsier than I actually was, I murmured, "What do you mean?"

"You were moaning," he said, and I could hear the dark suspicion in his voice, but he couldn't possibly think I'd made myself come. My wrists were chained over my head, and I was wearing a chastity belt.

"Dreaming," I whispered, feeling sad as the last wisps faded away.

The light flared on, and I heard Jack reaching for the keys. In seconds, I was undone, the cuffs off, the belt off, and Jack's warm fingers had spread apart my nether lips, feeling for the wetness I knew would prove my guilt.

"You came—" he insisted. "In your sleep. I know the sounds you make when you climax, Sam. Do you think I'm stupid?"

It was four in the morning. Yet Jack was completely awake. "No, Sir."

"What were you dreaming? Tell me quickly, before you can think of some fancy story."

I sighed and looked away, and Jack gripped my chin and forced me to face him.

"That you were punishing me—"

"How?"

"With your cane..."

"And did I touch you?" The look on his face was intense. I felt as if I were being interrogated at a crime scene, the bright light in my eyes, Jack's unsmiling gaze inches from mine. "Did I fuck you?"

4

"No, Jack."

"Did you touch yourself?"

"No, Jack."

"You came from the pain alone?"

"Yes, Sir."

"You're not lying to me, are you?" he asked, letting me loose and then leaning back against the pillows, contemplative. He was at ease now. A change had taken place, but I didn't know why.

"No, Sir."

"Describe the dream."

I huddled under the blankets, arms wrapped around my legs, and I tried to remember all the details. "I was wearing a thin white nightgown."

"Do you own one like it?"

I shook my head.

"Anything like it?"

"A sundress."

"Go get it."

I stumbled from the bed and opened the closet, then pulled a semi-sheer sundress from the rack. I slid the gown over my head, and Jack nodded his approval.

"Continue," he said.

"You told me to get into position."

"What position?"

"Knees bent under me, hands in front of me on the mattress, ass up in the air."

"Show me."

I looked at him, and he moved off the bed, slipping into the black pajama bottoms he'd tossed onto the floor. Jack often started the night wearing the pants, but kicked them off during sleep.

More nervous than ever, I pushed aside the comforter

and assumed the position on the mattress.

"What happened next?"

"You lifted my nightgown, so you could see my ass..."

"Why was I punishing you?"

"I—I don't know."

"Think."

I closed my eyes, and the whole of the dream came back to me. I'd been in a boarding school similar to the one I was creating for my novel. Girls were supposed to wear old-fashioned nightgowns and full-coverage panties to bed, and there had been a nightly check—done by Jack in my dream. When Jack had come to me, he'd discovered I had left off the panties. A cane had appeared seemingly from nowhere, as Jack had told me to assume the position and had caned me to climax, while the other girls gathered around and watched. Giggling. Pointing.

"Tell me," Jack insisted. "I think you know where we're headed. You don't want to make things worse on yourself."

So I told him. Cast him in the role of headmaster. Explained how I felt when he slowly dragged the fabric up my naked skin, when he revealed my lack of underclothes, when he started to cane me in front of an audience.

"And that made you come," Jack said softly, "that vision."

"Yes, Jack. Yes, Sir."

Jack walked to his cabinet and while my heart started to race, he removed one of his whippet-thin canes. Why couldn't I have come to images of riding on a Ferris wheel or being fucked on a blanket at the beach? Why couldn't I have told Jack I didn't remember? Jack dragged the dress up, showing off my naked skin. He pressed the

6

cane firmly against me, so I could feel the coolness of the implement, imagine how hot those stripes would be in mere moments.

"How many times did I cane you? How many times before you came?"

It was a dream, I wanted to cry out. *A dream, Jack! How the fuck do I know?*

"Samantha—"

"I don't know, Jack. I just came."

"We'll find out for ourselves then, won't we?"

He started then, before I could think, before I could speak, before I could even breathe. The cane cut into me once, and then almost immediately a second time. He was lining up the blows neatly, orderly, as Jack liked to do. I was still wet from the dream, still swollen from the climax, still lost in the confusing jumbled world of truth and make-believe.

"You'll wear panties to bed or pay the consequences." I felt my breath catch. He was playing. He was taking on a role I'd created. "I'm sick and tired of you breaking the rules. Thinking that sweet little smile of yours will get you out of trouble." And he was changing the script as he went. "I've let you slide before, young lady. From now on you'll feel my wrath each time you cross the line."

The cane slashed through the air, and I cried out, but at the same time, I felt the wetness of my arousal. Felt how turned on I was. Could I come again, solely from being caned and from the way Jack continued to talk to me?

"Were you touching yourself, girl? Is that why you had your knickers off?"

"No, Sir."

"You want me to believe you forgot them?" His voice was mocking.

"I don't know, Sir."

My head swam. Pain and pleasure floored me. And Jack continued playing, enjoying himself.

He kept up a steady monologue as the cane wreaked havoc on my skin. But I felt that climax building within me again, the pleasure managing to overshadow the pain.

"Bad girls are punished under my watch," he continued. "You'll meet me in my office in the morning, for a second dose... One delivered privately, so we can really get to the bottom of things..."

And that was it. All I needed. My pussy clenching, contracting. Stars in my eyes from holding my breath so long. I shook the bed, as I must have in my sleep, and Jack watched, almost curiously, until I was able to regain my sense of self. He didn't have to tell me what to do. I understood without a word of instruction, lifting my ass back in the air, preparing in case he wasn't finished.

He wasn't, of course. I'd gotten mine. Now he had his.

"Three more," he said, "Count them."

They were the meanest blows yet, the ones with his arm fully behind them, and I was shaking once more by the time he dropped the weapon.

When he was done, he kissed me. He brushed the tears from my eyes, bit gently into my full bottom lip. And then he climbed back onto the bed and pulled me to him, pressing me against his bare chest. His smile surprised me.

"Your dreams are my dreams," he said, then reached across my body and shut off the light.

Chapter Two:
The Perfect Girl

While Jack was at work one day, and I was putting the finishing touches on my novel, I heard the key in the front door. I knew somehow before the first footstep hit the hallway that it was Alex not Jack. And I knew something was up.

Alex was Jack's assistant. Young, attractive, blond, and completely dedicated to Jack. Usually, he was out at Malibu when we were in the city, or in New York handling business for Jack.

"You working?" Alex called out. I came to greet him, feeling suspicious. Alex was snarky as fuck. I can't say I liked him at the time, and I know he didn't like me. We were at the toleration stage. Barely.

"Yeah."

"Jack said you would be. Do you have time for a break?"

"For what?"

"Would you ask Jack that question?"

I took a risk. "No, but I'm asking you."

He tried to stare me down but failed. It was like the offer your parents always warn you about. *Hey, little girl. If you come with me, I'll give you candy.*

"I want to talk to Jack," I said, and Alex gave me another harsh stare, but I would not budge.

"He's in a meeting."

"I'll wait."

"He's not going to be pleased, Samantha." There was the threat. First I'd been given a promise of a reward. Now, I was being threatened with a promise of punishment. I sat on the sofa, implying with my body language that I wasn't planning on moving.

"What's gotten into you? Usually, you're such a good girl."

My radar was finely tuned. I crossed my arms and waited. Alex walked into the kitchen and dialed Jack on the phone. Then he called out to me. I headed to the bedroom and grabbed the extension there, and I didn't speak until I heard the click of Alex setting down the receiver.

"What is it?" Jack's voice was cold.

"Alex wants me to go somewhere with him. But he won't say where."

"And you don't trust him?"

"No, that's not it—"

"You don't trust me?" His tone was glacial now.

"No, Jack—" Uh-oh... What had I gotten myself into? "It's only that you didn't mention anything this morning, and I wasn't sure..."

"Right," he said, and the sarcasm made me flinch. "And I do run my schedule by you every day."

"No, Jack—" Jesus. I was floundering. "He wanted me

to go with him, but he wouldn't say why or where. And I wasn't sure you would approve..."

"...of my assistant doing as I asked him. Yes, I would see why that would make you suspicious."

My heart sank further. And when I thought of what Alex's expression would be when I headed back down the hall, I cringed.

"Are you in the bedroom?"

"Yes, Jack." And then, trying to redeem myself: "Yes, Sir."

"Bring the black-and-red paddle with you when you go back to the living room, and tell Alex I want him to pick up the phone."

Had I cringed before? Now, I bit my lip in pathetic despair. I'd thought I was tough. I'd thought I had a hand up on Alex. When in moments he would have one up on me.

"Alex—pick up!" I yelled. Then I held the phone to my ear for a second before Jack said, "See you tonight, Sam. Go do as I said."

Shamefully, I grabbed the paddle and headed down the hall to Alex, wishing I'd worn something other than the white-tiered skirt and formfitting white tee. Wishing I didn't feel like such an ingénue, an idiot novice, as I waited for Alex to hang up the phone.

"You could have simply said 'yes' when I arrived," Alex told me, snidely, emerging to slide the paddle from my grip. "You could have avoided this"—he paused—"this little unpleasantness." I'd left off cruel when describing him previously. Young, blond, and cruel. Trembling, I prepared myself.

Alex settled himself on the sofa, taking his time to get comfortable. He was like a baby Dom in training from

11

Jack. But he was good. I'll give him that. He enjoyed every fucking moment. I waited, rocking on my shoes, those insane white espadrilles that I never should have worn. They always brought me trouble.

"You know the position," he said, his voice soft now, almost crooning.

I nodded. I would not call him Sir.

"Then why am I waiting?"

I hurried to his side, and then lay over his lap, promising myself not to not to do something like this in the future. And yet a tiny voice whispered in my head: if I hadn't double-checked, if I hadn't called, wouldn't the same thing have happened to me later, over Jack's lap? It was a no-win situation, as usual for me. But as Alex pulled my skirt to my hips, as his fingertips worked my panties down my thighs, I realized that as always, even when I lost, I won.

Chapter Three:
Short Leash

Sometimes I sensed a difference in Jack, a holding back that I couldn't quite understand. He surprised me more often with interruptions by his assistant—Alex showing up unexpectedly at the apartment with something Jack wanted me to do. Alex driving by my favorite café when I was working—I didn't always spot him, but several times a week, I'd look up from my work to catch him cruising by.

Jack didn't trust me. That's what I realized.

I'd told him my history. I'd spilled my secrets. The darkest things that I carried with me. And yes, these confessions had made us closer. Had brought us tight together. But confessing to him also meant that he knew what I was capable of.

The crazy thing is that I'd always thought of myself as such a sweet girl. If asked to write a description, I wouldn't have put *cheat* in the top fifty words. Wouldn't have listed *heartbreaker*. But I could tell when I woke up to find Jack staring at me, or when I saw Alex drive by for the second time, that those late-night confessions had resonated somewhere inside of Jack.

Perhaps at first he had thought we were merely a fling. Perhaps it hadn't mattered to him at the start that I'd been with those other men while I was supposed to be with Byron. Perhaps…he was getting serious. And when you're getting serious you want to be able to know—know forever—that your partner would never, ever look at another man. (Or in Jack's case, not bend over another man's lap, or kiss another man's lips, or be whipped by another man, without his explicit permission.)

Don't get me wrong. Jack didn't treat me poorly. He wasn't ignoring me or disparaging me or trying to drive me away. Yet there was a space between us—even when his body was aligned with mine. There was a distance between us—even when we couldn't get any closer together physically. And I felt ice inside me from the sensation.

At first, my response was to show him how good a girl I could possibly be. I was there, every evening, when he walked through the door. Dressed in one outfit after another, all of his favorites. I had his whiskey in hand, like a '50s housewife, and I had toys spread out on the coffee table. So maybe not exactly like a '50s housewife—unless there were kinky housewives in the '50s—but docile and sweet, ready with "Yes, Sirs" and "Thank you, Sirs."

Jack seemed as wary of my new behavior as he had been of my old.

And Alex's drive-bys increased.

My next plan was to show him that I didn't care. He could mistrust me, question me, follow me if he wanted to. He wasn't going to catch me doing anything unexpected. I held my head up high, pretending not to see Alex. A *fuck-*

you attitude, I suppose, but one that gave me strength. Yet, I got bored with that. It's demoralizing to feel as if the man you love thinks you're a whore. And that's the feeling I got. Creeping in. Slowly. Easily. I started to feel as if Jack was simply waiting for me to fail.

I tried to approach the situation like an adult, telling him, "I'm yours." Over and over. "Only yours." Explaining. Pleading. "I don't want anyone else..." Still, I felt the mistrust. Felt it as if he'd put a heavy weight on me, around my neck.

I wouldn't fail him.

But I couldn't live like that, either.

When I'm unhappy, I can't write. So it became useless to take my notebook to the café. For years, I have run to clear my head. So I started driving down Sunset to the beach and running from Santa Monica into Venice and back again. I didn't even try to find Alex. I was sure he was there somewhere. But I ran, hard, every day, and then headed to the apartment to get cleaned up.

Then I went to a new café, one that didn't have so many open windows. This one would be more difficult for Alex to play his cat-and-mouse games. If he wanted to make sure of my surroundings, then let him show up in person. I took things a step further. I parked my car several blocks away, and entered an office building, choosing an inner door to reach the café, rather than the one on Sunset.

I did this for several days before Alex figured out where I was. He must have been searching the offices first, because finally he entered the café and looked around, spotted me in the corner, and let himself relax.

He came over without any sign of embarrassment, and sat at the table.

"You've been here every day?"

"Yeah."

"Why aren't you going to the other place?"

"Change of scenery."

"Why don't you run at the gym?"

"I like fresh air."

"No such thing in L.A."

"Why are you here, Alex?"

"You're a smart girl. Answer that yourself."

I looked into my coffee. "Jack doesn't trust me."

"He wants to know you're safe."

I met his eyes. "He doesn't trust me."

"Take that up with him." There was the sound of a dare in Alex's voice, as if he didn't think I would.

"Tell him you couldn't find me."

"What?"

"Tell him you looked, but you lost me. Again."

"Why would I do that?"

"Because I'm asking you to."

Alex regarded me for several seconds. "I don't understand your plan."

"You don't have to."

"Tomorrow," Alex said, "I'm going to tell him where you go each afternoon."

I nodded. "Fine."

He hesitated a moment before standing. "Don't fuck this up, Samantha."

"It's already fucked up, Alex."

"But not irredeemably. You can still fix it."

I grinned at him. He was a romantic at heart, wasn't he? I didn't need to make him squirm, although I kind of enjoyed the power. "Don't worry," I told him, "That's my plan."

Chapter Four

Wicked Game

Ah, now you're questioning me.

You think I'm one of those people who gets what she wants and then doesn't want it anymore. But that's not the truth. I wanted Jack more than anything I could possibly imagine. I was illuminated by the way we fit intricately together, the way Jack could read me. My wants. My needs.

Yet I couldn't stand the frightening distance slowly growing between us. I'd already lived in a war zone with Byron. And I'd wound up captured, a victim for years. This time, I would confront the situation with full force.

But I couldn't do it alone.

I may have acted as if I had no friends in L.A., no allies at all. Of course, that wasn't true. I'd met buddies at school and at the different salons where I worked. Mostly superficial, but a few I held on to. My best girlfriend was a manicurist to the stars. She'd painted the toenails of nearly every famous celebrity there is. Elizabeth was starlet beautiful—with porcelain skin and large cobalt eyes. Slightly taller than I am and sleek, she had hair that fell to the middle of her back. And although she'd have been flat-out gorgeous if she kept her natural hair color of pale chestnut, in reality, she was a chameleon. Working in a salon, she had easy access to hair dye and to the best colorists in the industry. One week, she'd be platinum blonde, the next—wham—she was a redhead.

Right now, to my great relief, she had hair as dark and glossy as mine. I called her up and explained a bit of the plan. She didn't understand everything, because I wouldn't give her the full details. (She would have been shocked if I'd told her the true story of my love affair with Jack.) But as a fan of noir films, she appreciated the concept.

The next day, Elizabeth came to the apartment as soon as Jack left. I gave her the keys to the car, dressed her in one of my standard running outfits, and had her put her hair back in a typical ponytail. Up close, we don't look much alike. But as a blur running by on the beach, she'd fool Alex for a moment.

I took a deep breath, scanning my surroundings. And then I grabbed a box of Hefty bags from a cabinet in the kitchen and started. In a few hours, I'd gathered up everything I owned. Every tube of lipstick. Every stray stocking. I didn't pack anything that Jack had bought for me. Only the items I'd arrived with. But I put away all of my treasured knickknacks, the bergamot-scented candles, the black-and-white postcards on the fridge. The space returned to the masculine, sterile atmosphere it had been when Jack found me.

The bags fit neatly in the empty closet of the spare room. If things went according to my plan, I'd be emptying them shortly. If not, well, I was already packed.

I'd told Liz to do my typical run then drive to the café

on Sunset. She didn't have to pretend to be me. She should get a coffee and wait. I explained that Alex would probably show up—and she didn't have to tell him anything. But if it was Jack who arrived looking for me—and that was the only thing I was worried about—then she should let him know I was at home, waiting for him.

When I was finished "moving," I took a shower and headed to the bedroom for the final preparation. I hoped I hadn't miscalculated.

The key in the lock let me know that someone was home. I heard the hesitation, heard the intake of breath. Knew that it was Jack. Not Alex. That Alex had fallen for my plan, and then, upon discovering Liz, had called Jack. That Jack had hurried home from work, thinking the worst.

He must have been surprised to see the way the place looked. I hadn't done all that much, but the little feminine touches had made a difference. I wanted him to know what life would be like without me, on the very basest of levels. I wanted him to miss me before I was actually gone.

I heard him walk slowly down the hall, but when he got to the bedroom door, he stopped. The door was almost all the way closed. Was he steeling himself for finding an empty room? After a moment, Jack pushed open the door, and our eyes met. And then there was silence. So long. So hard. It took everything in me not to fill in the blanks.

Finally, Jack said, "You want to tell me what the fuck is going on?"

"You start."

"It's your move, kid. You seem ready to call the shots. Who's the girl?"

"Friend of mine."

"She knows about us?"

"She knows enough." He waited, leaning against the wall now, and I continued. "She helped me out. Bought me time."

"For what?"

"This—" I hadn't dressed after the shower. I was on the bed, naked, and I'd cuffed my ankles and tossed the keys to the corner of the room, clicked the cuffs onto my wrists, and hung the chain from the hook on the wall. I was as exposed as I could possibly be. And deeply grateful that it was Jack in the room and not Alex. I didn't know if I could have handled this reveal twice.

"I don't understand."

"You don't trust me," I said, my voice soft, but unwavering.

"Sam—"

"You don't. You don't trust me at all. That's why Alex does his little drive-bys every day. That's why you've been pulling back from me."

"I haven't—"

"Jack." I said it in the same tone he'd said my own name, and it stopped him. "You have. You think about the fact that I was with those other men while I sported Byron's rock on my finger. What type of girl acts that way, right? You didn't care at first, because—" I stopped. I was guessing here. "Because you didn't know what we'd mean to each other. But now you're starting to like me, and you can't deal with the fact that I fucked those men and then slept in a bed next to Byron every night. You can't deal with the fact that I was a cheat, and a—"

"That's not—"

"It is. It can't be anything else."

He stared at me, and I felt his eyes roaming over my

20

body. "So what's the rest of this all about? Where's your stuff? Why are you cuffed like that?"

"If we can work past this, I'll stay. Otherwise—"

"You're threatening me."

"No. I would never. I'm telling you. I can't be here if every time you look at me, I see the word *liar* in your eyes. I haven't lied to you, Jack. I haven't cheated on you. I haven't." There were tears in my voice now, and in my eyes—"I wouldn't—I can't believe you think I would. That I could."

He came a step closer to the bed.

"But why are you cuffed?"

"I need to know. Is this how you want me? Is this what I need to do to show you that I'm yours? Stay here, naked, every day, cuffed to the bed. Nowhere to go. Nowhere to hide. Is that what you want?"

He shook his head. "Jesus, no."

"Or in a cage? Do you want to lock me in a steel puppy cage before you go to work? Have Alex take me out and walk me at lunchtime, then find me waiting with my head down, for my Owner at the end of the day?"

"I'm not your—"

"What do you want, Jack? What do you need me to do? How can I show you? How else?"

He was closer to me, and I could see the conflict in his eyes. He wanted to believe me. He wanted to so badly. "I trust you," he said.

"You don't."

"I do. I don't know why I had Alex tail you. I wanted to know what you were up to. I never thought you were seeing someone else. And then, when you started doing weird things, changing your schedule, going missing, that's when I got worried."

"Suspicious."

"Worried," he said. "Watch yourself. You don't know everything."

Jack was taking back control. I could feel it. He had made a decision—a decision that meant I could unpack. Once he set me free.

"You're pretty clever," he said, "going to all this trouble. Cleaning up. Hiding out. Making me worry." And then he laughed, that low, almost sinister chuckle. "But you fucked one thing up." I stared at him, waiting. "You cuffed yourself the wrong way."

"What do you mean?"

"I want you face down, Sam. Not face up."

He was quick with the keys then, undoing the ankle restraints, flipping me into the position he craved. "You play a mean game," he said, hand stroking my naked ass. "And you're pretty damn good. I'll give you that. But you know the rules. To the victor go the spoils."

As he went in search of his weapon of choice, I wondered who he meant. Had he won this round, or had I?

And did it really matter?

Chapter Five:
Wrapped Around Your Finger

Jack stroked me all over with his bare hands. Up and down. Not leaving any part of my body untouched. I'm trained as a masseuse, and yet I'm one of those strange creatures who don't like to be massaged. In fact, if I don't know someone well, I don't like to be touched at all. I don't hug people on greeting. I don't spontaneously hold hands with my friends. I have a history of being stand-offish in this way.

And yet...

When Jack used his bare hands to stroke from the tops of my shoulders down to my feet, he made me purr like a relaxed panther. My body was humming, electrified. He didn't tickle me. He didn't touch me too gently. He used firm strokes, over and over, until I felt as if I were flying.

Only then, after he'd put me into an almost hypnotic trance of pleasure, did he bend close on the bed, press his face near the nape of my neck, and say, "You worried me."

He'd lulled me, tricked me, created this false sense of

safeness in my surroundings, and now that was replaced by instant awareness. My skin prickled. My muscles tightened.

"On purpose," Jack continued.

His breath warmed the back of my neck, but I would not turn my head to look at him. I was frightened of what I might see in his cold blue eyes.

"I told you before," he continued in a menacing whisper. "I told you not to make me worry."

Oh, I'd been so pleased with my plan. And it had worked exactly how I'd hoped. But should I have confronted Jack in a different way? Spoken to him like an adult rather than playing behind his back? No... He understood this. He understood dirty pool. Christ, he was a lawyer after all. But that didn't mean I could get away free. Jack had to take back the power. And that meant I would endure the punishment he chose.

I could feel Jack's body against mine, pressing hard. He was still dressed, which made me feel more naked than ever. He straddled my body from behind, so that I could feel how hard he was, and I knew that I'd turned him on. He was like steel. Even when I'd made him worry, I'd managed to turn him on. We had a powerful connection, a type that rarely exists. You can meet people who will spank you. You can meet people who will tie you up, who will fuck you six ways to Sunday. But this was different.

Jack could read me.

"You're so smart," he continued. "What do you think I should do to you?

I held my tongue.

"I'm asking you a question," Jack repeated coolly. "You get two chances in my world. Name your punishment."

Like in the fairy tales. You know the ones. The Grimm Brothers' cruel tales—always my personal favorites. In which the evil queen or imposter princess is tricked into naming what ought to happen to someone who has behaved in the exact manner that she has. (The royals never recognize themselves, somehow.) But this was different. He would do what I said. And I was responsible for choosing the proper level of discipline. It would be like sending me out to cut my own switch. If I chose one too weak, too slender, I would be punished far worse than if I picked correctly from the start.

I knew better than to tell Jack to spank me. Spankings are candy to me, a reward more than a true punishment.

"I'm waiting."

Two things Jack didn't like: worrying and waiting. I was digging my hole deeper by the second.

"Crop me..." I didn't ask it as a true question, yet I didn't have the strength to make my voice a statement. The cadence was somewhere in between.

"Good choice," Jack said, rising from the bed and heading to the chest. "We'll start with that."

I tensed, automatically. I wished for clothes, even clothes Jack would lift or rip off me. Being totally naked is always worse. Always. Jack started slowly. Each stroke hurt, but I could tell he was saving his energy, and this scared me more than if he'd cut fiercely from the start. Jack had a plan. He might be pretending to put me in charge, but he was driving the car. He knew the route.

He used the crop until my ass was on fire and my breathing was ragged. Tremulous. Then he touched me once more. The same way he had at the start. Stroked me all over with his strong hands, making the pleasure radiate through me. Intense. Remarkable to feel such

25

sweetness and tenderness after such pain. And once more, even though I ought to have known better, I let myself relax, melt into the mattress, close my eyes.

Jack leaned over and, like the prince before the kiss, asked, "And what should your punishment be for trying to persuade Alex to lie to me—"

Oh, fuck—

"Did you think he wouldn't tell me?"

"I—"

"Did you really think so?"

I plead the Fifth, I thought, but didn't say.

"Name it, Samantha."

My head spun. My heart raced. What did Jack want to hear? What ought I say?

He pressed even closer, his body on top of mine, holding me down. "One last chance, baby. Name it—"

Chapter Six:
Under My Thumb

Did I really think Alex would lie for me?

Honestly, I didn't consider what I'd asked him to do as lying. Simply omitting. And that's different, right? Not to Alex, apparently. Or to Jack. I'd forgotten a key element in the relationship of our twisted trio—Alex reported to Jack. That was his job. And he lived for his job. Lived for Jack, as far as I could tell. This wasn't some office scenario with ever-shifting alliances. Alex was one of those guys who craved a role model. A father figure…

All of these thoughts swam through my head, like those signs in a Magic 8 Ball—the inky blue liquid cleared and slowly another message appeared.

But I didn't have time to process the dynamic between the two men in my world. I was face down on Jack's bed and he was waiting impatiently for me to name my poison. I tried to put myself in Jack's position. I knew better than to choose one of his toys, because that would be too easy. A crop was fine for transgression number one. But this was different. This was bigger.

"You write all day," Jack said, bending now to be eye level with me. "I know you have a creative mind. You ought to be able to come up with something perfect."

I write. That's true. But words come easier for me through my fingers than my lips. I can never ask for the things I truly crave. (A remnant perhaps of that night with Byron. The vodka-drenched midnight when I begged him to use his wood-backed brush on me, and he looked at me as if I were lower than something stuck to the bottom of his shoe.)

But suddenly, I had an idea.

"Untie me," I said, my voice feeling raw from lack of use. I'd been quiet so long.

Jack stared at me.

"Untie me," I repeated. "Let me have my notebook."

His eyes narrowed. He didn't like this request. Maybe because I didn't phrase the statement like a request.

"Please," I added, almost as an afterthought. "Please, Jack. Let me get to my notebook. I'll write down what I think you should do to me—"

"What you think you deserve."

"Yes, Jack," I spoke meekly now. "Yes, Sir."

He cocked his head at me, and I could see he was considering the offer. Art and life, blending together.

"A script?" he asked, and I knew he didn't want to star in something that I had penned, as if he were an actor, and I the director. No matter what we did, he needed to be in charge.

"No, Sir," I said quickly. "My penance."

Jack nodded. And smiled. He liked the concept. I could tell. He'd read my writing. All of it, I think. Not the way Nate had, each morning as part of our agreement. But for pleasure, chapters at a time. He never gave me feedback or comments, never had really mentioned my work until now. Telling me that I had a creative mind. Creatively kinky, but no more than Jack's.

He let me loose and then sat on the edge of the bed while I slid into panties, jeans, and a long-sleeved T-shirt. Casual, easy clothes for writing.

"You can't watch me work," I told him.

"You have a lot of demands."

"I won't be able to write if you're staring at me."

"Try it."

"Jack—"

He stood and looked at the clock on the nightstand. "You have an hour," he said. "I'll be back."

Like the witch in *The Wizard Oz* with her nasty hourglass. Sixty minutes. I hadn't expected that. I don't know what I had thought Jack would say. "Tomorrow." Or, "Whenever you finish." Of course not. But writing in a specific time period was new to me. Even if this was something I'd requested.

Jack left the room, and I could hear the front door open and shut. He'd left the apartment, as well. I sat down on the bed with my notebook, and I stared at the blank page.

Blank.

That was the perfect description of how I felt. I didn't have any idea of what I should tell Jack to do to me. I didn't have any idea what the standard punishment was for things like this in Jack's world. For inspiration, I crossed the room and opened the closet door, then started to paw through the contents. There were a variety of costume-style outfits: naughty nurse, prisoner of love, 1920s flapper girl. All sexy, sheer, short, and tight. And then I looked at the shelf on top of the closet—the rows of boots, and high heels, and marabou-tipped slippers, and...

At the end of the row was a bag I hadn't noticed before. A doctor's bag. I stood on tiptoe to take it down. Jack had never pulled this out before, and it had been tucked in such a way that I had thought it was simply another one of my many purses.

Inside the bag were various real-looking medical devices. I knew what to write about. I didn't know if I could handle what I was saying. Didn't know if Jack would even be into what I was writing. But the shame that filled me as I penned the words made me sure that I would at least get credit for effort. I wasn't going to stick to the same old style of punishment we'd played with in the past. Not a whipping—public or private. Not a session in his hateful puppy cage in Malibu. I spread out the various frightening-looking items and started to work. The stainless-steel speculums. The rectal thermometer. The rubber gloves, the old-fashioned enema syringe...

"She must be unwell," Alex, the assistant, murmured to the doctor.

"Yes, definitely. When she's feeling herself, she'd never act in such a naughty fashion." A deep sigh. "We'll need to do a thorough exam to determine the cause. It would be against my judgment to punish her until we know the cause for her malfunction."

"What are you planning?" Alex asked, fingering the different items on the sterile tray.

"You'll take care of the preparations. The enema. The shower. Record her temperature in her chart. And then I want her spread out on the table and readied for me."

"Yes, Doctor."

My heart was pounding. I'd written stories that skirted this issue before, but never really delved. Naughty patient, strict doctor. That's nothing new. But the thought of Alex assisting Jack made me wet. And the knowledge that Jack had been waiting to play with me like this—that bag up there, where I could find it at any moment—that let me know I must be on the right track. I crossed my legs tight and tried to continue. But in my head, I could already see Alex stripping me of my clothes, handing me some flimsy little tie-in-the-back nightie. Caring for me intimately at the instruction of—and I had to say it, at least in my mind—his Master. Because Alex was as much a slave as I was.

That thought stopped me. Just because I said the words didn't make them true. I had to consider the concept. But it made sense. Alex didn't simply punch a clock. No normal job required an assistant to spank a boss's girlfriend. My head swam, and I tried my best to return to my story. One that I knew would be less fiction and more reality in a matter of minutes. Could I handle that?

I realized that there was no "me" in the piece. Not yet, anyway.

"Call her in."

The patient entered the room, head down, cheeks flushed pink.

"You know the rules," the doctor said, his voice stern, but calm. "Lying is a serious offence. But before you're properly caned, we'll need to make sure that you're fully capable of withstanding the punishment."

Oh shit. Properly caned? Where the fuck had that come from? I crumpled the page and tossed it on the floor, then repacked all of the devices in that black medical bag and tucked it away once more at the back of the closet. I had to work a little to make the top shelf appear undisturbed, and I was sheened with sweat by the time I sat down on the bed and started again.

What if I simply said that Alex should spank me for asking him to lie to Jack? He could bend me over one of the chairs in the living room. He could use his belt. That would make us even, wouldn't it?

I started to write once more. As quickly as I could. The clock was ticking. I'd wasted precious moments going through the closet for inspiration. Had wasted more time on that fucked-up Doctor fantasy. Now, I did my best to capture a scene Jack would appreciate. He'd never watched Alex spank me. He'd probably get a thrill out of that, right?

"Bend over the chair, Sam. Hold tight to the arms."

"Lift her skirt," Jack instructed. *"And pull her knickers down."*

"Of course."

Alex's fingers gripped the waistband of Samantha's lipstick-red panties and dragged them down her thighs.

"Step out of them, kid," Jack instructed. *He was in charge. Even if Alex was doing the punishing. He was always in charge.* *"And hold still, doll. It's going to hurt. Right, Alex?"*

"Yeah, Jack. That's the point isn't it?" A low laugh. *"Why bother if it's not going to hurt?"*

Samantha lowered her head. She bit her bottom lip. She could hear Alex undo the buckle on his belt, could hear the almost nonexistent sound of the leather being pulled free of the loops. In total silence, she waited for the first blow, wondering how many he would give her, how much it would hurt, how long she would manage to take the pain without crying—

The front door opened. I glanced at the clock. Oh Jesus. I was out of time. How the fuck had that happened? I kept on writing. Jack's footsteps down the hall spurred me on. I had nearly a full page of text by the time he pushed the bedroom door open. He took the notebook from my hand and read, his eyes following the text quickly. And then he handed the book back to me and picked up the crumpled piece of paper from the floor. As he spread the sheet out flat and began to read the discarded story, I saw a smile light his blue eyes, and I realized I was like those idiot imposter princesses in the fairy tales.

I'd named my punishment. Ordered my poison.

And now I would have to drink.

Chapter Seven:
Secret Things

By now you know that I think sugar tastes better in cubes, that coffee is richer in my favorite mug, that food is more luscious on a special blue glass plate. I am focused almost as much on presentation as I am on content, which is why I worked so hard to fulfill this fucked-up fantasy scenario.

Jack didn't want me as a patient, though. Instead, he had me dress as a nurse in a crisp white uniform, so short you could see the tops of the white lace garters. White stockings. White, stack-heeled, patent-leather pumps. The outfit had red piping, like icing, on the seams and the pockets, and the stockings each sported a red line down the back that was almost impossible to keep straight.

I dressed in silence and solitude, imagining Jack in the other room discussing the situation with Alex. Who would do what. How long they would torment me. My hands were shaking, and I was in no position to put on my makeup. But I worked hard. After slicking my hair back into a neat ponytail, I outlined my full lips a dark ruby and then filled them in. I was still admiring myself in the mirror, when Alex opened the door.

We didn't take this thing to the moon. Alex wasn't wearing a white lab coat. Didn't have a stethoscope hanging around his neck. He looked more like an intern than a doctor. At first, that is. But when I met his eyes, I saw a gleam there. He was pleased. This had worked out to his benefit. He'd remained true to Jack the whole way—and now look. He was being treated like a prince, the heir to the throne.

I wondered why Jack had even asked me to bother getting dressed, because Alex roughly tugged the snaps open on the outfit without a word, letting the sterile white dress fall open. He admired my matching pearly white bra and panties, before indicating that I should lose all three: dress, knickers, push-up bra.

Alex watched as I stripped, and heat stung my cheeks. I'm no stripper. I have none of that inner confidence you see with women who work the pole. So that's why Jack had instructed me to put on this uniform. Because it almost hurt to undress under Alex's hawk-like gaze. Only when I was down to the garters and heels did he take a step forward. I felt faint as Alex spread me out on the bed, as I realized with a jolt that the mattress had been covered with a new sheet. A rubber sheet. Must have happened when I had been in the bathroom. My heart pounded and my head swam.

This was my fault. Why hadn't I come up with some other sort of fantasy punishment? I'm a creative person, after all. I might have penned any number of kinky scenarios...

As I continued on this self-pitying trip, Alex was preparing something behind my back. I should have been paying attention. Isn't that the story of my life? I should have been preparing myself. But how could I? How could I possibly?

Alex didn't say a word. He didn't have to. He simply arranged me how he wanted me on the bed, on my hands and knees, then had me lean forward with a pillow under my chest, rear raised. For a moment, I thought (I'll even say I hoped) that he was getting me set for a spanking, that the rest of the fantasy would remain simply that—a fantasy. But why would I have such little faith in my man? Jack had been saving that doctor's bag for a reason. A reason, a motive, a perfect time.

Sliding one knee on the bed, Alex moved closer to my body. His hand gently began stroking my lower back, and I wondered if he meant to relax me. I was so tightly wound, I felt as if any motion might shatter me to pieces. And then, my worst fears realized, Alex dabbed something slick around my rear hole and slowly began inserting what felt like cold metal between the cheeks of my ass.

I was horrified. So filled with shame that I closed my eyes tight enough to see violent purple stars. Slowly, water began to pour inside of me. There was no pain involved. Alex wasn't hurting me in the slightest—in any way except my ego. I knew my cheeks were beyond scarlet. This punishment stemmed from the fact that I'd asked him to lie. He wasn't only punishing me at Jack's request. He was doing so as a reward for his own good behavior.

I didn't have much time to process these thoughts, however. Most of my effort went into not begging, not pulling away, in properly behaving in spite of my total misery.

When Alex was finished, and I was well filled, he slid

a plug easily inside of me, patted me once on the ass as if I were a house pet, and left the room.

Oh Jesus. How long would he leave me like this? What was he waiting for? Was Jack going to come and view me in this utterly humiliating position? Was Alex going to come back? I started to cry, tears streaking my cheeks, but I didn't call out, didn't move at all. Finally, Alex came back to the room. When I looked over my shoulder, I saw the glee on his face. He was wickedly enjoying every second of my absolute, overwhelming discomfort. Yet he didn't say a word. He simply lifted me in his arms and carried me to the bathroom, and then, to my great and utter relief, left me alone.

There were instructions for me. To remove the plug myself. To expel the water. To shower. And to know— in Jack's own words—that this was only the beginning. I tried not to think about what that meant as I followed the commands. There was a timer on the sink. I had sixty minutes to myself. And I relished every one.

When Alex came back for me, he didn't offer me clothes. He pulled my towel off and let me walk down the hallway on my own. Barefoot this time. Totally naked.

"Face down," he said, first words I'd heard from him since we'd begun. "Wrists over your head."

I obeyed, and he bound me quickly, easily. Being tied down made the rest somehow more bearable. I didn't have a choice anymore. I *had* to take this. And then that soft knowing voice in my head whispered, *You deserve it. You named your punishment, and look at you now.*

This time I watched over my shoulder, watched as he removed a thermometer from the doctor's bag. Watched as he got out the lube and moistened the tip. He set the thermometer on the edge of the dresser, then slid on a pair of rubber gloves, slowly, knowing I was clocking every step.

Then he was behind me once more, slipping in the device, holding it in place. The same shame filled me, and yet—my body was responding. I hated the fact that I was wet. So fucking wet. That being probed like this, clinically, without any apparent emotion, was turning me on.

When he had removed the thermometer and recorded the number on a notepad, he returned to the doctor's bag and removed a type of speculum I'd never seen before. The keywords of this evening seemed to be *ass play*. Once more, I felt the smear of lube between my cheeks, and then the total chill of the metal tool entering me, penetrating me. Alex worked slowly, carefully, spreading me wider and wider. And then his fingers were inside of me, stroking, petting, so that the sensations of pleasure and hopeless humiliation warred a private battle within me. If he kept doing that, would he make me come? I wondered what would happen if I did. Nobody had told me that I shouldn't enjoy myself during this little performance. Again and again, Alex fluttered his fingers between my spread cheeks, until I shuddered, right on the bridge of climax—and that's when he backed off. Pulling his gloves off his fingers with a resounding snap.

"I'll call in Jack now," Alex said. I could feel how wet this examination was making me, but the thought of Jack walking in, of Jack seeing me like this, made me more aroused yet.

Jack chuckled as he entered the room. He liked the sight immediately, and I registered the fact that the doctor's bag was probably going to be at the forefront of our toys in the future. But it would be different to play only with Jack, wouldn't it? The true shame came from having Alex carry out his Master's commands.

"Has she behaved?" Jack asked Alex, his eyes still on me.

"Yes," Alex said honestly. Thank god. I'd thought for a moment that he would lie, to pay me back.

Jack's fingers were on me now, closing the device, sliding it free. I felt gaping without it. Empty.

"Lovely," Jack said. "So on to the reward."

"Reward—" Alex repeated. "But—" He seemed hesitant to disagree in any way with Jack, and yet he had something to say.

"The cane, of course," Jack continued, and I shut my eyes once more. Was being caned a reward? Not like spanking. Not like the feel of Jack's worn leather belt on my skin. The cane was something else. Something that took me to an entirely different place.

"Five," Jack said. "I'll watch."

It was Alex who was going to whip me. Ah fuck. So now I got it all. I understood. I shouldn't have tried so hard to behave, thinking that would win me points. I could have begged him not to go through with the enema. I could have kicked and screamed and acted the regular brat the whole time and the result would have been the same. The reward was for Alex, not for me.

"Count them," Jack said, coming closer. "Count them out loud."

"Yes, Sir."

"And thank him for each stroke."

I swallowed over my hatred for the cruel blond Baby Dom. "Yes, Jack."

Jack lifted his chin in a silent gesture toward Alex, and I heard the swish in the air before the cane connected, and

I sensed the moment of impact for a second before I saw the blinding red light of total pain.

"One," I managed somehow. "Thank you."

"Sir," Jack instructed.

"No—" The word slipped out before I could stop it. Before I could think of what the repercussions might be. Alex wasn't *Sir* to me. He just wasn't. But I could have pretended I was talking to Jack. I could have played a trick on myself. I could have...

"Let's say ten," Jack said, stroking my hair. "We'll tame our little outspoken filly yet."

The cane landed a second time, and I shut my eyes tight. "Two. Thank you." There was a naked pause in the room. Everyone was waiting for me. "Thank you, Alex."

Jack stepped forward then and grabbed the cane from Alex's hand. It was a blur of movement as he landed three strokes on the fleshiest part of my ass before I could even process what he was doing.

"You're disobeying me," Jack hissed. "I've told you what I want."

Once more my face was wet with tears, but I looked at him dead on. I wanted to talk to Jack without Alex in the room. Jack could sense that. But he took his time before he told Alex to wait in the hall. Then he bent close to the bed.

"He's not—" I started. God, how to put this in words? "He's not you. He's not the same as you." Almost sobbing. "He's not your equal. I don't want to call him Sir."

Jack smiled at me, startling me. "Yet you're disobeying an order."

I didn't know what to say to that. I had no response.

"You'll say, 'Thank you, Sir,' after each blow."

"No."

We were at the same place we'd been in the New York club when I'd refused to give my safeword to a Dom I didn't consider my own. I'm a stubborn animal when I want to be. I wouldn't say Sir. And Jack, after regarding me for a moment, seemed to realize that. His eyes took on a glow.

"Ten extra for disobedience."

I grimaced but nodded as Jack let Alex back into the room.

Chapter Eight:
Modern Love

Pain takes me to a different place. The sensation of being whipped, or cropped, or caned elevates me to a state that meditation (and probably self-medication) takes other people. But I have to be steeled inside to get there. Jack had Alex cane me—*properly* cane me, as I'd written in my own damn story—and then he uncuffed me, rubbing my wrists where the silver metal had chafed the skin.

There was silence in the room. Both men watched me.

Trembling and tear streaked, I still understood what Jack wanted. What he expected. Eyes down, I went on my knees before Alex on the cold wood floor. Head bowed, I found it within myself to apologize for asking him to lie for me.

"I'm sorry, Alex."

"A bit more," Jack demanded. "I'd like a bit more—"

I wasn't meeting Alex's eyes. That was the problem. "I'm sorry," I said again, looking up at him. "I should never have done that, Alex."

He had his half-smile, a smirk really, in place on his handsome face. As difficult as I was finding apologizing to Jack's second in command, the boy was loving every fucking moment.

"A bit more," Jack continued, and now I was at a loss. I looked up at him from my position on the floor, and my eyes widened as I saw Jack give Alex a nod over my head. What was going on? When I glanced back at Alex, I saw him working his belt buckle open.

No—I didn't say it. Sometimes I'm smart. But I thought it—*No. I don't want him to use his belt on me. I don't want any more. All I did was ask Alex to lie. That wasn't such a huge offense, was it? I might have done so much worse. If anything, they'd gone over the top in teaching me my place. Jack could have washed my mouth out with soap. Could have let Alex simply spank me. Could have done so many other...*

Christ, he was pulling the belt free now. I'd written two scenes. Was that what this was about? Jack had chosen that crumpled-up piece of paper, and I'd assumed he was discarding my second attempt. Clearly, he had put the two together in his mind, recreating my work as a good editor should.

"Over the bed." Alex was the one to say it.

No—my head said again. But my body obeyed. My body was better trained by now than my brain. I climbed into position, tense to see if Jack would cuff me once more. He didn't. And somehow that was worse. There was no talk about how many I'd take. There was no discussion of thanking the Dom-in-training behind me. There was only leather and skin, and my harsh breathing, and Jack watching. Because Jack loved to watch.

Alex didn't put his full force behind the blows. I could

43

tell. But that didn't mean he went easy on me. He heated up my skin everywhere the cane had missed, and he intensified the fire where the cane had landed, until I was wrecked, my head on my bent arms, my body shaking with silent sobs, and that's when Jack moved.

I had my eyes closed. I didn't know what was happening. I simply felt the air still around me. Knew that the thrashing was over. Could feel Jack's sturdy weight on the bed, his body behind me. Then against me. He was hard. Probably had been hard since the first snap was popped open on my nurse's dress, simply thinking of me in this room with Alex. I visualized him out there in the living room, scotch in hand, imagining Alex touching me, examining me with those slick rubber gloves in place. Had Jack worked himself while he thought of the fantasy coming true down the hall? Or had he waited, growing harder by the moment, knowing the pleasure would be so much better if he didn't give in right away?

Now, there was no reason to hold back any longer. He slid into me, and relief flooded through my body.

Too soon, of course. Too soon.

Jack gripped my heavy hair in one hand, pulling my head up, and I saw Alex in front of me. Alex stripped down. Alex, with his cock right in front of my lips.

I slid backward on the mattress, moving closer to Jack, who kept his hand even tighter in my hair. Was this how he really wanted me to apologize? Or was this my reward?

"Do I have to tell you?"

"Yes."

"Apologize," Jack said calmly.

"I'm sor—"

"With your mouth."

Alex moved closer, but my lips remained sealed.

Jack's cold laugh was more of disbelief than anything else. "Don't test me, kid. You don't want to see me get mad. I'm not sure you could take my wrath tonight." His words let me know precisely how upset he'd truly been with my underhanded ways. And I started to think that perhaps this whole scene was only the beginning. Jack had much more in store for me. He always did.

I clenched my eyes shut tight. I parted my lips. I tasted the head of Alex's cock for the first time. Jack didn't stop fucking me. If anything, he rode me harder, slamming his body against mine, so that I had to work to keep steady, work to suck Alex in a pleasing, easy rhythm. My thoughts raced as my body struggled for some sense of balance.

Was this what Alex had wanted the whole time?

Had he ratted me out in hopes I'd be presented to him on a platter?

Or was this scenario a long time coming?

Had Jack always known Alex would ultimately be introduced into our bed?

Alex pressed forward, taking control of the rhythm, fucking my mouth now, as Jack fucked my body. Jack let go of my hair, and the long curls fell forward around my face. He was using both hands on my hips now, rocking me, grinding inside of me. His palms on my heated skin simply turned me on even more. Jack knew me so well. As the action between the three of us built in intensity, he began slapping his hands on my ass. Not hard enough to make me cry out, but hard enough to show me he was in control.

Of course I didn't doubt that for a second.

Alex pumped his cock between my lips over and over,

and then he tensed, and I pulled back instinctively and closed my eyes. Jack must have watched Alex come in my hair, on my face, and that took him to his limits, jerking my hips back against him, sealing himself to me...

Chapter Nine:
Always Falling

"Phone's for you," Jack said, and his eyes narrowed. So I knew right away it was a man.

"Who is it?"

"You tell me."

I'd known from the start that life with Jack would be the antithesis of my experience with Byron. Jack had told me what he was about from our very first date. He'd explained step by step what he wanted to do to me, if I'd let him. You couldn't get much clearer than the description he'd offered. Jack didn't play head games. Not in the way that Byron had. Yeah, sure, Jack mind-fucked me. But in the most deliciously sexy ways possible.

What was missing from our relationship?

Arguments. Byron and I fought all the time. At least until I stopped arguing back and simply let the verbal abuse rain down on me. In the months before I left Byron, I walked around our house as if there were a constant weight on my shoulders. I felt unbelievably lighter when I moved out.

Stress. There was none. Jack had his job—which had been his life before me, as far as I could tell. And then he had me, and when he was home, he was focused. Attentive. Interested without being intrusive.

So when Byron tracked me down, looking for a second shot, I was floored. Had he not lived in the same environment? Had he enjoyed the tension, the live wire of constant anxiety that illuminated our townhouse? I remembered one night when he wanted to "have a talk" with me. But we had to attend a function at his father's mansion first. Knowing I was in trouble made me jittery. And being jittery around two hundred people in fancy clothes made me drink. Every tray that passed provided relief. I don't know how many glasses of champagne I managed to swallow before Byron realized what I was doing. I do know that I spent the night in one of his father's guest bathrooms, curled up on the cool marble floor between the toilet and the bidet. That night perfectly illustrated our life for me. I wondered what image did it for him.

"Hello?" My voice was tentative, as I was aware of Jack's eyes on me.

"I'd like to have to lunch," Byron said, no preamble. No small talk.

"Why?"

"See how you're doing."

Jack's eyes were pure ice. I put my hand over the phone.

"It's Byron," I mouthed. "I don't know why he's calling."

Jack leaned against the kitchen counter, watching me. This had become a test. I could tell.

"To see you," Byron said, and his voice didn't seem so confident anymore. He sounded hoarse. I thought back to our last fight, when he'd told me that Los Angeles wasn't big enough for the two of us. As if he were some gunslinger from the Wild West.

"I can't," I told him.

"I know who you're with," he said, and his voice hardened into a sneer now. "Jody told me."

I shrugged, but of course he couldn't see that. I didn't look over at Jack now. I wanted to get off the phone.

"He's bad news," Byron said, "watch yourself."

"Thanks for the advice," I said, my tone matching his. "I have to go." And I handed the phone back to Jack—remembering as I did that there were friends who had offered the same warning about Byron. Bad news. He was edgy. He was dark. In real life, he was a mama's boy.

Jack led me back to the living room, hand on my wrist rather than on my waist. I felt the chill coming off him, and I knew he was displeased, even though I'd done nothing wrong—in my opinion, anyway.

"What'd he want?" Jack asked, as he sat on the sofa, sitting me on the edge of the coffee table in front of him.

"To see me."

"Really?" Jack's eyes weren't cold anymore. They were on fire.

"Jack," I started, "come on. I didn't do anything."

"Where'd he get your number?"

That was easy to guess. "He worked for Jody. He entered his whole Rolodex onto the computer. I'm sure he had a backup at his house. You've been to parties at Jody's place. You're listed in his database."

"Why'd he want to see you?"

"I don't know." I was feeling nervous now, guilty. But that didn't stop me from adding, "I'm not a mind reader," which was obvious from the look on Jack's face. Had I been a mind reader, I would have known not to be flippant. Not to push my luck.

"Why do you think?"

"Because Byron likes to spread out all of his choices. He's probably hooked up with his old girlfriend. And now, when he's getting ready to commit, he's making sure he's through with me." I said this from experience. When Byron and I first were dating, he had done the same thing. Gone through a slew of women before he committed to me.

"Through with you…" Jack echoed. "I thought you were the one to break up."

My head was spinning. He was turning my words around in his neat lawyerly way. "Come on, Jack," I said again, pleading now. "I don't want him. I wasn't going to see him. I hope he never calls again."

Jack stared at me, leaning back on the couch and regarding me as if I were a piece of art he was interested in purchasing. He stood up and left the room. I heard the front door open and shut, and realized he'd left the house.

Oh Jesus. I didn't know what to do. Race after him? Or wait for him to return? Beg him to believe me? Or act as if I didn't know why the fuck he was angry? But I did. Someone had managed to infiltrate Jack's world. Had managed to throw off his balance. And Jack couldn't stand that.

It was after midnight by the time Jack came back. I was in the same place as when he'd left. I had tricked myself into believing that if I didn't move, if I stayed exactly where I was, then everything would be okay.

He walked into the darkened room, but he didn't turn on the light. Instead, using the lights from Sunset, the neon glow, he walked toward my silhouette, came behind me, put his arms around me. He kissed the back of my neck, then slowly unbuttoned my shirt and slid it off me. He took off my bra next, his fingers deftly working the clasp. He pushed my skirt down my hips, hooking my panties with his thumbs. I lifted up, so that he could take the clothes all the way off me. And then I was naked, sitting on the coffee table, with Jack behind me, his breath on my bare skin.

He didn't say a word. Gently, he ran his fingertips along my shoulder blades, then down my arms, raising goose bumps all over my body. He kissed me, tenderly following the route of his fingers. I expected him to switch into high gear at any moment, expected him to grab me up, carry me to the bedroom. Or to bend me over the sofa or his lap. I thought he would punish me for the phone call—regardless of the fact that I hadn't instigated the connection with Byron and it wasn't my fault.

But Jack surprised me. He did grab me up, but instead of taking me to any of the places I'd thought, he spread me out on the rug I'd bought, a soft crimson rug. Spread me out on my back and settled himself between my legs. He was still fully clothed, and he sported a rough five o'clock shadow, and I was naked and splayed out in front of him. Jack took his time; he parted the bare lips of my pussy, opened me wide, and then used his fingertips and tongue in the same manner he had when I was seated on the table. But now he employed this trick on my pussy. His fingers trailing in circles and diamonds, his tongue tracing over those same dangerous designs.

I closed my eyes and lifted my hips, silently hoping that he wouldn't stop. That he would take me to the edge. Take me past. Take me over. He rubbed his face against the tender skin on the insides of my thighs, and I groaned at the way his whiskers scraped against me. And then he was back. All softness. All sweetness. His tongue on my clit, tapping now, rapping, until the pleasure flooded over me, through me, and I couldn't help myself. I gripped his shirt with my hands and held him to me. Crying out. My voice harsh, as rough as the feeling of his evening beard on my skin.

Sighing, I leaned back again, but Jack didn't stop. He continued to trick his tongue between my nether lips, knowing not to touch my clit directly now. Giving me time to recover. I started to moan, not even aware at first that I was making any noises at all. Helplessly crooning under my breath. He brought me to the brink again like this, with tongue and fingertips, cresting, teasing, until I started to beg him...

"Please, Jack—"

Beg him louder.

"God, Jack, please—"

And now Jack sat up and looked down at me. The light through the glass doors was red tinted and colored our skin. He didn't speak; he simply stared at me and then started to pat my pussy with his hand. Light little taps. I arched to meet his hand, my brain barely processing the moment when the taps grew sharper, stronger, when the love taps turned to spanks. My hips rocked back and forth on the rug, and I shut my eyes tight.

"Look at me," Jack instructed.

Automatically, I opened my eyes.

"This is what you need," he said, stopping all contact. I was on the verge, so fucking close to coming that I could taste the pleasure.

"Please, Jack—"

"Say it."

"I need this—"

"What do you need?"

"You."

He smiled. It wasn't the answer he'd expected, but I could tell it was acceptable. His hand came back down, building in the rhythm, the intensity, until I was coming, hard, fast, breathing as if I'd run a 10K, and then Jack was stripping quickly and fucking me on the floor, the rug pushed away, so that it was hard wood under us. Jack's body slamming into me.

After, he grabbed up the soft cashmere blanket from the sofa and wrapped us in it, neither of us having the energy or the will to make it to the bedroom.

I knew we'd both be bruised in the morning.

And I knew that's what Jack wanted.

Chapter Ten:
More Than This

Anyone in a true Dom/sub relationship knows that there are times you *want* a spanking (and oh, how you want it, wiggling your ass each time you pass by your lover, hoping he or she will notice), and times you *need* one. Unfortunately, in my experience the two situations don't always coincide. I can only say it's like craving an attitude adjustment. Sure other people deal with their shifting moods in completely different manners—working up a sweat at the gym, yelling at underlings at work, swearing at drivers on the freeway. I like my way better, but that doesn't mean I always like to be spanked.

Jack, as you can guess, could read my moods with an almost frightening ability.

I wrote my second novel quickly and signed immediately for my third. My editor had slid me into his girl/girl line. He'd read the many lesbian scenes in my first novel and liked the way I wrote them. I didn't mind being pegged as a lesbian writer. I penned all sorts of scenarios for the short stories I was publishing, and I slipped in other scenarios in most of my books.

I don't get writer's block. Not in any extreme way. I've trained myself to stop working on a project if I'm floundering with it, and to move on to something else. This is probably one of the reasons I'm rather prolific. I always have a slew of stories in progress, and novels under construction, and I switch tracks quite easily from one to the other.

But I had a day—a crazy day—when I know that if I'd been working on a typewriter the floor would have been littered under my feet with crumpled-up white paper. This is because there are songs in this novel. I'm somewhat proud of the lyrics I created, but they came under great duress. I'd never attempted to write words for a song before. I have such intense respect for actual songwriters—what they do is astounding to me. The poetry of the words matching with the perfect melodies—I can't begin to explain my awe. I am no songwriter. That became clear after my seventeenth attempt to write the lyrics for one song in my book.

Jack came home to find me in a truly black frame of mind. He'd never seen me like this before. I hate to say that I'm a perpetual optimist. Rarely do I fall into true funks. Even when I was depressed during the months it took for me to break up with Byron, I managed to have happy days. Sweet moments.

Jack observed me in silence as he had his first drink of the evening, watched me stomp around in my heavy blue Docs, grumbling to myself. I wasn't late on the deadline. But I'd wasted a day. I hadn't taken my own standard advice of pushing the work aside and moving to something else. I hadn't tried my basic trick of going for a run on the beach or even on the rubberized gray treadmill at Jack's gym. Instead, I'd fallen in deeper and deeper. And, fuck me, I was beyond rational thought by the time Jack entered my mood.

He walked around me, catlike, avoiding me. I'd said hello when he entered. I wasn't a total idiot. I didn't need to spark his wrath. But I couldn't put on a smiling face, couldn't tie on a false frame of mind like a lace apron around my waist and play happy housewife.

He let me be for over an hour, and then he called me into the bedroom. I'd been reading and rereading my notes, growing even more despondent about the likelihood that I'd be able to make this thing work. And then what? Would I have to go back to the beginning? Would I have to scrap the concept completely?

Oh...god...

"Samantha," Jack called, and I sighed, not wanting to get up from the desk, and not wanting to spend another fucking second staring at the words I disliked so intensely. "*Now!*" His voice had been warm, welcoming, even. But at my hesitation, the change was immediate and intense. I could feel the cool air all the way to the spare room. And like an animal aware of a predator, I realized what I'd done.

During the day, Jack had called, and I had been curt. Bordering on rude, even. I'd told him the situation, but I hadn't asked him about his day, hadn't been able to shake myself out of my mood even for a moment. As I headed toward the bedroom, I felt myself coming back to the present. For the first time all day long, I was able to leave the worries of my work behind. Because the worries of what Jack was up to surpassed them.

When I got to the bedroom, I felt my mouth go dry.

There was Jack, waiting. Jack, ready. Jack was dressed in a black T-shirt, a pair of black leather pants, and black boots. He wasn't dressed like that to stay in—I could tell. He looked imposing and menacing in a manner I rarely saw. More serious somehow because of the severity of the outfit.

On the bed was his favorite of my schoolgirl skirts, so short that you could practically read the back of my day-of-the-week panties (if Jack allowed panties to be worn). He had chosen a plain white blouse and a black cardigan, and a pair of high-heeled patent-leather Mary Janes with ankle straps. White fishnet thigh highs completed the look. There was a bra but no panties on the bed. But his belt was coiled up next to the schoolgirl uniform.

"When we're finished here, you'll get dressed. I don't want to be late."

"Finished—" I echoed, feeling the dismal mood slowly draining out of me, replaced bit by bit with a fresh wave of fear.

"You don't think I'm going to let your behavior today go unnoticed."

I hung my head.

"Not rewarded, of course," he continued. I heard the dark smirk in his voice, yet I knew that had I looked up, his face would be stone.

"No, Jack."

He didn't tell me what to do next. He took over, coming forward and placing me roughly against the wall, palms flat to keep myself steady. He worked the buttons on my fly before hauling my jeans and panties down for me, just past my knees. His belt was already off, and he had easy access, was able to grab it up, double the leather, and start without hesitation.

Each stroke felt impossible to bear. I don't know why or even how the pain can fluctuate—or maybe it's my ability to take the pain; maybe it's the mood that matters. But I was in that place, that bratty, mule-headed place, and I lost my head. I tried to turn, to tell him—what? To tell him no? That it wasn't fair? That I hadn't done anything specifically to him? I'd been in a funk because of my writing. That was all.

But none of that counted. My mood had bled into Jack's world. And that's all that mattered to him. That and the fact that I tried to fight the punishment, which changed the situation for both of us.

He was on me now, dragging me over to the bed. And I fought him, not wanting to get away—not really. If I had been desperate, I would have acted differently. We both knew that by now. I would have groveled. Begged. Wept. Instead, I tested him, struggling, and he had to work to get cuffs on me, to pin me down the way he wanted, ripping my jeans and panties all the way off and going to work on my ass seriously now, blow after blow, until the struggling subsided and I was...

What was I?

I was...tamed?

No. Never tamed.

Broken?

No, not that either. Jack didn't want to break me. He liked me wild and spirited.

Fixed. That's how I felt. Back to normal. As if he had given me a dose of some strong medicine. Jack knew. I don't know how he knew. He knew because of who he was and who I was. He'd said he'd known me since he'd first seen me at Jody's party, years before. He'd claimed he understood me way back then. Now he'd known—in himself, in his heart—that I was craving this sort of treatment. The fighting on my part was merely a last desperate struggle to hang on to a foul mood. Why would I want to do that?

When he was finished, we were both breathless. But I was me again.

Jack kissed the nape of neck. Then bit into my shoulder through my T-shirt. He didn't tell me not to behave in this manner again—as he had when I'd worried him with my absence. I think he understood he would come home from time to time and find me craving a tune-up, the type only he could give. He kissed me again, then undid the bindings and left the room, waiting for me to dress in the outfit he'd set out, giving me no other hint as to what was to happen next...

Chapter Eleven:
Hate Me Today

Jack took me to a private club, a members only environment deep in the heart of Hollywood. I'd done the club scene for years. Byron and I were extremely busy when we dated. We rarely stayed home more than one night a week. As a result, I've seen hundreds of concerts from Parliament to Neil Young to the Red Hot Chili Peppers to Marianne Faithfull in locations ranging from the Roxy to the Hollywood Bowl to the Forum. We often went to clubs to see friends' bands, or simply to soak in the scene.

But believe me, we'd never been to a club like this.

The place had been in business for years—decades?—and was dedicated to those with a penchant for BDSM-type play. The club's special rooms were available to rent hourly, with racks, punishment chairs, and examination tables. The place boasted multiple dungeons and hosted special nights, purposeful parties.

Had Jack been reading my novel in progress late at night, after I fell asleep? I'd set part of the book in a similar type of club. But mine was created mostly from imagination—and wishful thinking. Had Jack decided to give me a burst of reality in order to lend authenticity to my book? Or was it a coincidence, an overlapping of life and art that made me feel even more connected to my man?

On this night, Jack explained, there was a costume party. That was why he'd chosen the most extreme of my schoolgirl outfits, one that could not be mistaken in any way for an actual skirt. The thing was so short that it hung like a sash around my waist. Jack had given me a pair of Thursday panties before we left the penthouse, but that didn't provide me much relief. Especially when I saw the rest of the girls heading into the club. Most were wearing much less clothing than I had on—which made me think that by the end of the evening I would be missing the majority of my attire.

Jack greeted several of the other partiers by name, and then led me forcefully through the lush rooms of the club toward what I discovered was one of the multiple dungeons. This one, Jack whispered to me, was an Inquisition-themed room, and featured a variety of wicked ways to bind a naughty slave in place. We were early, I believe, and had the room almost to ourselves. Jack wasted no time choosing the device that he wanted, binding me with my arms overhead to a black metal bar, my legs wide apart. He'd left me in my full schoolgirl costume, and while I thought he'd start to play with me—if not punish me, then at least tease me—I was wrong. After firmly binding me into place, Jack not only didn't touch me, he left the room.

I'd gone from being Jack's meek partner, following along through the place with my eyes down, not making contact with any of the other guests—to being put on display and left alone. My cheeks flamed, and I wished

I'd had the intelligence to at least ask Jack what he had in mind. Most likely he wouldn't have told me, but I could have attempted to gather information. The not knowing was always the worst.

Jack came back in the room, and he wasn't alone. He had Alex with him, and now my heart—which had been racing—seemed to stop dead in my chest. *What the fuck?* Hadn't I been punished enough at Alex's hands? Did I have to accept a public flogging to pay for my sins as well? I lowered my head, feeling somewhat ridiculous in my bright-crimson-and-black-plaid skirt, my stark white fishnets. Most of the others I'd observed had been dressed in the standard black I'd witnessed at the two fetish-style clubs I'd been to previously.

I expected Alex to step behind me, expected some sort of repeat of the scene I'd gone through in New York. Would he ask me for my safeword? Would Jack be forced to protect me once again? I had no intention of letting Alex get the better of me, which meant that I needed to prepare myself to accept a flurry of blows without flinching. But I also knew that in this situation, Jack would have better control. He could stop Alex with a motion, with the nod of his head if he wanted to.

Except...when I looked up again, surprised at the length of time that had passed since Alex and Jack had entered the room, I saw something wildly surprising. Jack was binding Alex in place, face down, on a huge cross-like structure.

I was both excited and confused by the prospect of what was to come.

Alex had been wearing a simple black outfit, expensive, I was sure. He was like a mini-Jack, sometimes. Not in physical appearance, with his wheat-blond hair, but he took his cues from Jack—from the clothes he wore to the watch he favored to the wallet he chose. Not as high-end as Jack's, but the same clean, elegant style. When I'd been looking downward, Alex must have stripped off his shirt, for he was clad only in black pants now, and his leather boots. The fine muscles of his back were exposed, his strong arms bound into place.

What the fuck? I thought. *Oh Jesus. What was going on?*

Jack stood behind Alex, and he had a flogger in place. My mind tripped over itself in a mad rush to explain the situation. But my pussy didn't need any explanation. I grew wet at the sight, as I realized I hadn't seen Jack in action like this before. Not outside of gazing into a mirror while he punished me, making me watch while he tanned my ass for me.

This was different. Jack was in charge of someone else's pain. Someone else's ultimate pleasure. Have I ever felt such a surge of white-hot jealousy before? I can't think of a time. My stomach twisted, but my sex responded as strongly as if Jack had picked up a flogger and walked toward me.

Alex didn't say a word. Didn't make a sound. Jack leaned forward so that his strong chest pressed firmly against Alex's naked back, and I could imagine the words he was whispering in Alex's ear. I told myself that this was about me—about Alex being unable to tail me proficiently. But that was only the story I made up for myself. I had no idea what the true dynamic was between these two men. I'd come into their game late. Alex had been working for Jack since his senior year in college. They had history I couldn't begin to unravel.

Jack took a step back and started to work, and I saw

Alex's muscles tighten and release with each blow. The room was starting to fill up as more guests arrived. There were a host of devices in the room, and I could hear different sounds as other slaves were buckled into place, or whipped, or chastised. But that was white noise to me. I was focused, intent on the action right before my eyes.

Too intent, it turned out. Because before I was aware of what was going on, a queenly platinum-blonde woman in tight black satin stepped in front of me. She gripped my chin in her hand and forced me to face her. I tried to pull away, wanting to watch now as Jack dropped the flogger and reached for a crop. Some other little minion nearby undid Alex's belt and dropped his slacks. And oh, I wanted to see that.

The woman, displeased that I had not paid her proper attention, slapped my cheek hard and I broke from my daze.

"Jack's asked me to take care of you," she explained, her voice cold. "While he's busy."

I nodded, quickly, trying to catch up with the script that seemed to be moving in fast-forward. Alex was groaning. Not loudly, but loud enough for me to hear. I really wanted to know what Jack was saying to him. The burn of jealousy intensified, and I would have wept had the lady before me not forced my focus on her deep-green eyes. Fake green, I saw immediately. Too emerald to be true.

To my horror, she released the cuffs and the bindings holding me in place. She was going to take me somewhere else, somewhere away from Jack. I pulled back from her immediately. No thought of what might happen. No consideration of who she was, who she might be. I could not leave Jack and Alex by themselves—even if they were "by themselves" in a room of people. I wanted to see how Jack touched Alex afterward. Would he be gentle with him? Would he wrap Alex in his arms? That thought made me want to double over, my stomach clenched.

The woman was not someone to mess with. I should have understood this by the fact that she'd slapped my face within seconds of "meeting" me. She gripped my hair in her hand and pulled back hard, and in seconds, she had assistants at her side, two men who crowded close to me. They didn't touch me. But their sheer size was intimidating. I looked from her to the men and then back to her again.

"Jack has asked that we take care of you," she said, and her voice was lulling now, as if she intended to quiet me, the way you'd soothe a spooked animal. "Will you come on your own?"

I looked at the men, looked through the gap between them to Jack and Alex, and I felt myself digging in my heels. Quite literally. I was going nowhere until Jack told me to. They could drag me out, and I'd cause a scene, and maybe that's what people around here lived for, but I'd take the risk.

"Jack has to tell me himself," I said, and I saw a glimmer of something in the woman's faux jewel eyes. A flicker of understanding. She touched one of the men's shoulders and nodded, and he headed over to where Jack was now methodically cropping Alex. I could see the marks, the welts, and I felt a shudder work through me.

There was a hushed conversation out of my earshot, and then Jack leaned against Alex once more, and I knew in my head he was promising pain, more pain, in a moment. Then Jack was at my side, and the lady and her enforcers gave us space. "They're to get you ready for me," he said. "Don't worry so much."

My eyes pleaded with him. "I want to stay, Jack."

He shook his head.

"I want to stay." I couldn't make myself say, "I want to watch," because that hurt too much somehow. But I couldn't bear to leave Jack's side.

"They'll take care of you." Jack's hand stroked my cheek exactly where the lady had slapped me. So he'd been paying attention—at least, peripherally, perhaps in the mirror on the rear wall—even while he'd been working over Alex. "I won't be long."

And I lowered my head and let the lady grip my wrist and take me down the hall...

Chapter Twelve:
Jealousy

I can't describe the intensity—the blood-red anger, the black wave of jealousy—I felt at watching Jack whip Alex. It was worse than if I'd caught him kissing someone else. Worse than if I'd watched him in the sweetest embrace. I wanted to pull the crop from his hand, to make him stop, to drag him back to my world. My face was hot, and when I pushed the hair out of my eyes, I saw that my hand was trembling.

"This way, Samantha."

Somewhere in myself I knew I could leave. I could always leave. If I didn't like what was going on, that was my ace in the hole. Jack didn't own me. He couldn't stop me. If he wanted to be with Alex, be Alex's Master (oh, the thought sent a wave of nausea through me), then let him, right? I could walk.

But the ties went deeper than that.

"This way," the woman repeated, and I knew I wouldn't run. Knew I was committed. I couldn't be broken that easily. Or that I was broken too much already. Too shattered to flee.

"Now." Her voice, slightly cajoling at first, had hardened, but it wasn't until Jack turned and looked at me once more that I let myself be led from the dungeon.

I felt as if I were in a dream—a fantasy come to life—as the lady took me through one room after another. We moved quickly past pictures in motion—images that would normally not only have captured my attention but made me so extremely aroused I would have had a difficult time taking a single step. The majority of the girls I'd seen upon entering the building were subs like me. I could tell from their attitude and attire. Some were now over their owners' laps. Others were being led around by leash and collar. Still more were being punished in the same sorts of ways that Jack was currently taking care of Alex. But it seemed as if the women employed by the club were nearly all Dominatrixes, and they stood out boldly in their sexy outfits, painful gear in hand. Some putting on shows for the crowd. Others simply mingling. You could tell these women from the rest because their outfits were all made from the same black satin cloth as the outfit worn by the lady leading me through the festivities.

Yet, although I processed bits of what I saw, my mind was focused on the activities in the room I'd been led from.

What was Jack going to do to Alex next?

And why the fuck couldn't I watch?

The chilly blonde moved me through the throngs easily. People deferred to her, stepping back out of her way. I'd thought she was queenly on first sight, and that image remained. She led me without speaking until we reached a door at the end of a hall, and here she took a key on a chain around her neck and opened the lock.

Inside was a private bondage room, much like the one at Jack's place in Malibu. But even more intricately designed. As Jack's had been decorated by Alex—my guess, of course, but that's what I was fairly sure of—it lacked a woman's touch. This room was done in extreme detail. There was sumptuous fabric on the wall, rich scarlet and midnight black. A glass chandelier hung from the center of the ceiling, casting diamonds of light throughout the room. Roses stood in a vase on a white marble pedestal. Their fragrance was strong and heady enough to reach me in the doorway. Ivory candles burned in several corners, enhancing the atmosphere, yet I also saw strategic electric lighting placed throughout. You could have as much or as little light as you wanted in this environment.

The devices on display were as frightening to a newcomer as any I could imagine. But truthfully, I've never gotten over the first shock at seeing furniture intended solely for the binding of trembling limbs. Gear created with the purpose of inflicting pain. There was a large steel chair that made my legs weak—a chair with straps to hold ankles and wrists, with a place to bind a collar around a slave's neck. Across from the chair stood a spanking bench. Nearby was a leather-padded examination table. In one corner of the room dangled a cage suspended from the ceiling. A wardrobe stood with doors open to reveal what appeared to be every cane ever created, every type of crop, quirt, paddle...

"Jack's asked that I prepare you."

I turned to look at the lady, her words awakening me from my daze. I was seeing this room, yet still lost in the vision of Jack punishing Alex. Was he trying to spare me by sending me away? Was he worried I would be unable to take the sight? That I would break down?

Whatever happened, I promised myself, I would make Jack proud. I stood a little taller at the thought, my back straight, my head up. Proud for the second or so I had until the lady at my side said, "Take off your clothes."

And then I was scared once more.

At my hesitation, she moved forward, her hands on my cardigan, pulling it off me. Her fingers working the buttons on my shirt. I felt two shadows enter the room and saw the men she'd been flanked by earlier. The large, well-muscled men. Why were they here? There was no way she'd need their power to subdue me. She had six inches and a good forty pounds on me.

Her hands were rough, ripping my skirt off, until I was wearing only my white bra and those day-of-the-week panties, thigh-high fishnets, and heels. I knew better than to cross my arms over my chest, to hide myself in any way. With every bit of inner strength I had, I stared into her eyes.

The nearest man immediately grabbed my arms, pulling them behind my back and forcing me down to my knees. "Show your obedience." He sounded more amused than angry, as if my naïveté was somehow charming.

I realized that my goal of being strong and proud had failed. I was to show this lady the same deference I would show Jack. And the look I'd given her was anything but submissive.

From my spot on the floor, I saw the woman's foot come forward, clad in a lace-up, high-heeled granny boot. I didn't need her goon's hand on the back of my head to know that I was to go forward, to kiss the toe. I did so automatically, realizing this put me in a completely open position. My ass rising up in the air as my head came down. She laughed at my display. Perhaps experienced slaves show their submission more easily than I did. Or perhaps she caught the joke of Jack giving me Thursday panties on a Friday.

In an instant, she had pulled me upright, and was quick-stepping me to the spanking horse. I didn't fight, and she laughed again—this time for the audience of her two sidekicks, I was sure. "Jack said she was spirited," she said. "But she seems plenty docile to me."

Had I failed already? I wanted to please Jack. I wanted him to come in here and have the lady tell him that I'd done what he said, and yet my good behavior was winning me no points. Did he want me to fight her? Struggle with her? If he did, it was too late now. The woman had already gotten me in place, binding my wrists herself then kicking apart my legs so that she could fix my ankles.

Then she started, paddle in hand, meeting my ass with sure, stinging strokes. She began strong, yet managed to build in intensity, and the pain ricocheted through my body. Again and again she let the spanks rain down, and I gasped for breath, but did not moan. Did not cry out. I played games with myself—I told myself she'd stop at twenty, and then counted backward with each blow.

Three.

Two.

One.

But of course I was wrong.

I pretended Jack was the one spanking me, and that worked for another few strokes, imagining my man wielding the paddle, doing my best to behave for him. But then my mind turned to Jack and Alex—and I started to lose myself.

Alex hadn't cried out. Hadn't even seemed to do more

71

than flinch as the crop connected with his naked skin. Was that why Jack had made me watch? Was he my model? Was I supposed to learn from Alex?

The paddle slammed against me, and I closed my eyes, tears streaking my face, as the lady forced me to pay attention to her. I felt cold metal against my thigh, as without a word, she slit the sides of my panties and pulled the fabric free. Then she laughed once more, and I knew she was admiring the stripes left by Jack earlier in the evening—god, it felt like years ago that I'd played the role of the brat.

Jack had definitely managed to erase that mood, hadn't he?

The woman was on me once more, this time with a new paddle against my bare skin. I could hear the eerie whistle before the paddle connected, and I knew she'd chosen one drilled through with holes. Jack owned a similar paddle at home. I shut my eyes tight, I bit my bottom lip, and I braved my way through the punishment—thoughts of Jack and Alex and the whole world driven from my mind by the pain.

"No begging," the woman whispered when she was through. "Impressive. Jack's spoken so highly of you. But it's nice to see for myself."

Her words sent new ripples of fear through me. When did Jack speak to her? Did he come here often without me? Who was she to him?

My head spun with problems for which I had no solutions.

No answers.

And then I felt a change in the room, in the very temperature of the place.

Jack had arrived. I could tell.

"She ready for me?"

"Of course."

"Did you tell her what to expect?"

"I thought you'd rather it be a surprise." The woman's voice held a musical note, as if she were flirting with a good friend.

"Just as well," Jack said, and he sounded as if he were smiling when he responded. "I can take things from here..."

Chapter Thirteen:
Pain of Love

When Jack and I were alone in the room, he freed me, undoing the bindings on my wrists and ankles and returning me to a standing position. He put his hands on my shoulders, steadying me on my crazy-high heels, and then he spun me around and stroked my well-warmed rear.

"Juliette is a pro, as always," he said, and I could tell he was admiring the fresh color of my skin. I stayed as still and quiet as I could, my mind positively screaming with questions for him.

Why had he made me leave the room?

Why bother having me watching in the first place?

Did he want me to know that he truly was Alex's Master, a concept I'd always secretly thought?

But more pressingly—prepare me for what?

Faced away from Jack, I thought of the various devices in the room, and I tried to guess which one might bring Jack the most pleasure. Would he place me in that scary chair? Or stretch me out on the padded table? Or...

Jack went on his knees and parted the cheeks of my ass, and I sucked in my breath. I reached forward, straining for balance, wanting to at least place my fingers on the spanking horse. But Jack wouldn't let me fall. I knew that. He spread the cheeks of my ass and licked between them, and all thoughts and all fears momentarily disappeared, replaced solely by the intensity of pure pleasure. By that kinky sort of pleasure of being touched there. And knowing what that touch meant for my future.

The door to the room wasn't fully closed. I remembered that. Jack had walked in and taken over from the arctic blonde. But he hadn't pushed the door shut behind her after she'd left. Anyone could walk in and watch. Anyone could see what Jack was doing to me. Which was spreading my rear cheeks wide and licking around my hole. Around and around, with tantalizing slowness, knowing exactly what the sensation was doing to me.

Because fuck, I was floored by the bliss. The shock of it was almost numbing after swallowing the physical pain of the paddle and the emotional pain of watching Jack whip Alex.

After raising me close to climax, without letting me come, Jack stood and led me to the padded table. This was his choice. But he didn't bind me down. He simply pushed me against it, and I felt him behind me, working his slacks open, releasing his cock. He'd gotten hard punishing Alex—that was no surprise to me—and he was ready for release. Without hesitation, he slid into me, hard from the start, pounding me against the leather table. Slamming into my ass with the same intensity that Juliette—I had a name for her now—had paddled me.

I was breathless in moments and so turned on I could hardly stand it. The table pressed against my clit in the most delicious way with each forward thrust, and then I closed my eyes as Jack gripped into my hips and groaned, sealing himself to me, fucking me over the edge so that we were coming together—coming hard.

He pulled out almost immediately, tucking himself back into his slacks and regarding me from a foot away. I stared at him over my shoulder, feeling undone and exposed. I was wearing only the fishnets now, and my bra, and the heels, and I felt as if I'd been through some sort of sexual battle. Soiled. Used. Demolished.

And yet...my mind was working.... *That can't be what he meant when he asked Juliette if she'd prepared me. There must be something else. Something more.*

Jack walked to the wardrobe featuring the range of gear, and he stopped in front of it. My heart sped up at the sight of him regarding the different toys and tools, but then he bent down, doing something I couldn't see. And then Juliette and her minions were suddenly in the room—had Jack pressed a button? Given them a signal that I'd missed?—and Jack nodded to them.

"Come with me," Juliette purred, leading me into an adjoining bathroom I'd missed before. The door was covered with the same luxurious fabric as the room itself. A hidden door. I wondered how many of those secret entrances and exits existed in the club. I entered meekly after her, and she nodded toward the shower, turning on the hot water for me. "Clean yourself up. I'll wait."

This room was as well designed as the one we'd recently left—a lady's boudoir, with a lounge for Juliette to relax upon, a vanity mirror, a breathtaking array of perfumes and fancy soaps.

While she watched, I kicked off my shoes and pulled down the stockings, then removed my bra. She nodded toward the sink and I saw a basket filled with hair accessories. I pulled my long hair into a ponytail then stepped into the steamy shower.

When I emerged, Juliette was still there, holding a cherry-hued towel. She dried me off, and I waited, humble still, wondering what was going to happen next. Would she give me new clothes? I hoped so but didn't ask.

She didn't say a word now, simply led me back into the room, where I saw that Alex had been brought during my absence. He was a sight, stripped down himself, and positioned on that chair—the one I'd been praying didn't have my name on it. The thing was a cruel-looking bondage device, and Alex's wrists and ankles were firmly attached to the arms and legs of the chair. He had a collar in place, and this was attached to the neck of the chair. He'd been allowed more dignity than I had, however. He still had on his boxers.

I felt weak at this image of him, the Baby Dom transformed into a sub. Alex didn't look at me once. His eyes were fixed on the floor in front of him. I saw that his cheeks were as blazing red as the roses in the corner. And—I hate to say it, but that made me pleased. I wouldn't feel sorry for him. No matter how humiliated he must be feeling.

Jack wasn't in the room, but Juliette's male assistants were, and at her beckoning, they came forward. I was entirely naked, but not in the least bit cold. This room was more than comfortably warm.

"You heard what he wants," she said, and I realized that the room had changed in my absence, and not merely in the fact that Alex had arrived and Jack had departed. The cage, previously hanging from the ceiling, was on the floor, and the door was open—and I knew that Jack wanted me inside of it.

I backed away, into Juliette's waiting arms, but rather than hiss at me, or demand that I obey, she stroked my hair, breathed her warmth on the back of my neck, and brought her arms around me.

"Don't fight," she said. "It will be so much worse if you fight."

I understood the intelligence in her words, but the advice still didn't make me want to obey. I'd been in a puppy cage one time at Jack's, and the thing scared me more than any of Jack's other toys.

"You know you'll end up in it," she said, her voice low, intended for my ears alone. "But if you fight, you'll have to go through so much punishment first. Why not behave? Why not get into the cage like a good little mousy?"

Her words flowed over me but didn't sink in. I pushed back against her, my mind reeling for solutions. Where was Jack? If he entered the room, I could talk to him, tell him to bind me to the spanking horse instead. Or down on the table. Or to chains I'd noticed suspended on one wall. He didn't have to put me in that cage.

But "telling" Jack—that wouldn't work. I couldn't "tell" Jack anything. Not in this sort of situation. My lack of clothes made me hesitant. I didn't want to sprint through the club like a streaker. Yes, the partiers were in various states of undress, but a naked woman fleeing through their numbers would definitely cause a stir. And I could imagine what would happen to me. I'd be caught— undoubtedly, and probably easily—and I'd be put on display, used as one of the models for how to properly cane your sub.

I still hadn't taken a step forward, and the men hadn't moved toward me either. But we weren't at a true impasse. They could force me into the box with no problem—we all knew that. Clearly, Jack hadn't asked that I be put in the cage, but had wanted me to climb into the thing of my own accord.

"Alex didn't fight," Juliette whispered in my ear.

And that was all I needed to hear.

Chapter Fourteen:
All Alone

Closing my eyes now, I try to recall how I managed to make myself get into that frightening metal puppy cage. Maybe it was what Juliette had said: Alex didn't fight. Perhaps it was the fact that Alex was right there, his eyes on me, silently watching my every move, willing me to fail. I sensed that he wished I would cause a scene. My disobedience would make him look more superiorly submissive, wouldn't it? Alex, I could tell, always wanted to be the top boy. He needed the gold star on his forehead, the A+ on his chest.

Feeling his eyes on me, feeling the heat of the hulking men waiting to use force, I made a decision. They wouldn't have to tell Jack I'd failed yet again. They'd be able to offer a report of model behavior.

Still, looking at the cage, I had doubts. It seemed smaller than the one at Jack's house, and that had been small enough to cause a wave of claustrophobia to douse me in its embrace.

Somehow, I climbed inside, feeling the bite of the metal against my naked skin, a shiver running through me, both from that cold steel and from the sound of the cage door being shut. I wasn't bound. I was free—yet boxed.

Juliette gave me a smile, and I wondered whether she had thought I would fight. Whether I had behaved unpredictably in my obedience, or like a lamb led to slaughter. Docile and meek. Nothing I was doing this evening felt entirely right. Inside myself, I believed I should never have left Jack and Alex. I should have pulled a tantrum in that first room, forced Jack to deal with me, yanked his attention away from his assistant.

The two burly men came forward at Juliette's nod, and they lifted the cage easily and hung it from the suspension system in the ceiling. So now I was up. I was in. I was captured. What was going to happen next?

The two men left the room in silence, and I gazed down at the space. Why did Jack want me out of reach? Why did he want Alex bound in place?

Jack entered the room moments later, shutting the door firmly behind him. His hair was wet, so he must have showered, too, and he appeared relaxed and ready to answer those questions—if not with words, then with actions. My eyes were focused on him as he took in the view with a sweeping gesture: one slave bound in place, the other overhead. He smiled his pleasure at Juliette and then stood back from her and watched as she slowly undressed. And now the shivers grew more pronounced, running up and down my spine. I had a feeling what was going to happen, and I didn't want to be right.

I met Alex's eyes for a second, and he looked as horror-struck as I felt.

Juliette slowly removed her black-satin attire, stripping down to a fancy corset, dark-blue lace that hugged her form. She was curvy, her lush breasts pushed up by the device, her slim waist held in tight. Beneath, she had on a matching cobalt garter belt, inky black stockings, and spiked heels. She wasn't wearing panties. Jack ran one hand over her bare shoulder, and I felt as if he were touching me. Felt burned by the familiarity of the stroke.

What the fuck, Jack? I wanted to cry out. *Why do I have to watch this?*

Yes, Jack had watched another man punish me—but that had been fuel for Jack's own private fantasies. I'd never craved the reverse, hadn't spent my nights longing to see him dominate another female. I wanted to be Jack's one and only. I'd accepted Alex—somewhat grudgingly— but I didn't want a girl in the mix.

I realized that we'd never discussed the true rules of our relationship—other than us both accepting that Jack ran the show, and I was allowed my freedom to write. I knew that if I fucked around, it would be the end. But we'd never talked about what Jack did in his spare time. What he might be doing. What he had done before we met.

He knew my whole history—from my first date in junior high through my last fuck on Nate's bed. And I didn't know anything. Had he been married? Had he always been a rock-hard Dom? Watching him with Juliette brought all sorts of questions thrashing to the surface. And yet I couldn't spend time thinking about them, because he was busy now, binding her down to that maroon-leather table, fixing her wrists over her head, spreading her ankles. When he touched her between her legs, I moaned, and Jack looked up at me, for the first time. He didn't smile. He didn't wink. He seemed curious as to my reaction.

How was I dealing with his kindness to another female? Not too fucking well.

I hated the fact that he'd whipped Alex. But I hated this even more, despised seeing him touch her. Worse still, of course, was the fact that I was wet. Who wouldn't be aroused at the sight of a stunning ice-blonde princess, her ass in the air now, her body prepared for what I could only guess?

"You tell me," Jack said, loud enough for his voice to carry, but sweetly somehow, softly.

"A crop." She turned her head away when he went rummaging through the antique wardrobe, like a kid avoiding the view of the doctor preparing a shot.

Jack was in fine form tonight, wasn't he? First he'd taken care of Alex. Now, he was preparing to punish this pretty minx. What did he plan for an encore?

My heart raced as Jack ran his fingertips over the various weapons. He hefted one, then another, then returned to the table, his choice made. "I should have forced you to pick for yourself," he told Juliette.

"Send me out to cut my own switch?" she was teasing, her voice rising up at the end, but I caught the undercurrent of fear there.

"Exactly," Jack said. "You of all people know which one of these inflicts the most pain."

"It's not the tool, Jack," she responded, and she was smiling, although weakly. "It's the power behind."

She was right. I knew that. A whipping from Alex was entirely different than one from Jack, even if the same paddle, crop, or cane was used. The Dom was what mattered. Not the device.

I knew Jack had whipped Alex for the situation with me. For failing somehow, being unable to provide Jack with the information he craved. Basically for a job not well done. But I had no idea what the relationship was between Jack and Juliette. They seemed to be friends. I squeezed my eyes shut at the thought. I didn't want Jack to have female friends. I wanted him to be all mine.

I hadn't thought Jack was paying me any attention. He'd only looked my way twice. Now, he said in a voice that carried to me, "Open your eyes, kid."

Was he talking to her, or me?

I looked down, and we made instant eye contact. Powerful. Burning. He was talking to me.

"You watch," he said next. "You see how it's done."

Had I thought I was at the lowest I could get? Being forced to witness Jack's banter with this blonde? Being held captive overhead, like some exotic bird on display? Now I felt as if he'd put me underground, my heart in my stomach. He was going to demonstrate how one properly accepted punishment. And this...this...oh, whore, for want of a better word, was going to be his model.

Did that mean I had failed him as Alex had? Did that mean that when he whipped me, or cropped me, when he used a paddle or his belt, he was unhappy with my response? The thought made me sick to my stomach. I was being taken to school.

Juliette had on no panties, only the garters and the corset top. Her ass was a blank canvas for Jack, and he went to work. An artist if nothing else.

He didn't tell her how many. He didn't make her say why. He simply started, the crop cutting into her tender flesh, and she immediately barked out, "One. Thank you, Master."

At least she didn't call him Sir. "Master" had the same effect on me as the word had back in the New York club.

It signaled a false interaction, a make-believe scene. Jack wasn't her Master. Not truly. This was some paid-for advertisement, created solely for Alex and me. Punishment for Alex in some privately excruciating way. A lesson for me on how to behave.

I listened to Juliette count for him. I watched the stripes line up on her skin. I saw the change come over her when the pain grew intense. When she had to force herself to keep up the model behavior, shaking the hair out of her face, quivering in that instant before crop met skin, knowing how much it would hurt and working to prepare herself to accept that pain. I had the feeling she would be wet now; if I were to run my fingertips between her legs they'd be drenched in her sweetness. I had the image of doing exactly that, of soothing her somehow, and the concept floored me.

Not because she was a woman. I'd been with Ava, after all, a similarly cool ice blonde who invited me into her bed with her roommate and indoctrinated me into the exotic world of a girl-girl-boy ménage. No, I didn't have a problem with Juliette because of her sex, but because of her easy relationship with Jack. I wanted to hate her. I wanted to ridicule her in my head for her dyed platinum mane and her faux-emerald eyes. Yet, as I heard the sound of impending tears in her voice, I felt pity.

And, yeah, I also felt turned on.

So much so that the metal of the cage didn't bother me anymore. I spread my thighs apart and pushed down, gaining contact with the cold steel against my clit. I wondered how long Jack would keep me up here. If he didn't let me down soon, would my sex juices begin dripping to the floor?

Chapter Fifteen:
Vicious

If he fucks her, I'm going to rock this thing out of the ceiling.

That was my sole thought.

I can watch him crop her. I can watch him inflict the pain that she seems to crave. But I will not be able to watch him take her.

When Jack was done, he dropped the crop and undid Juliette's bindings. I stared, hands tight on the metal of the cage, not even feeling the chill of the steel any longer. I watched because I couldn't look away. Not like Alex, who was bound with his head faced forward, with no choice at all but to witness the unfolding scene. No, I watched because not knowing would be worse than seeing the drama with my own eyes. Juliette stood, shaky and laughing at herself for being off balance. Jack leaned back, waiting for her to speak. I saw him in my mind with a cigarette dangling from his lips, insolent in that James Dean pose. I saw him regarding her under half-shut eyes, waiting for her response.

"Not fucking bad," she said, and I knew that if I had said the words, he would have slapped me. Hard. Jack must have been thinking the same thing.

"You let your subs talk to you like that?"

"I'm not your sub, Jack."

He grinned at her, his expression softening. "I know."

I understood the sensations working through her. She'd gotten the pain. Her nerves were strung tight. Now, she needed the pleasure. I hated the fact that I was watching all this like a member of a silent audience. Yet there was no way for me to interact.

Juliette disappeared for a moment through the door to the boudoir, and when she was gone, Jack focused his attention on Alex, undoing the bindings, setting the boy free. Alex was stiff from having sat in a forced upright position for so long, and he stretched slowly, his eyes on Jack. He appeared wary, as if wondering what Jack might have in store for him next, and he didn't seem to be prepared when Juliette reemerged, fully dressed in all-black once more, silky pants and a long-sleeved sweater.

"You don't mind, do you, Jack?" she asked, gripping on to Alex's wrist.

Jack shook his head.

"I'm so hungry after a tune-up like that."

And now Jack nodded, and I could see Alex's face lose a bit of the worry. Had he been here before, with Juliette? Did he know what future pleasures awaited him? She opened the door to the room and pulled him after her down the hall. Jack shut the door behind them.

I watched, still feeling breathless, gripping the cage, scared beyond measure. Jack surprised me. He climbed onto the leather table and stared up at me. Regarding me now with the same look he'd given Juliette.

"What are you thinking?" he asked.

I swallowed hard. It felt like years since I'd last spoken. "I don't know."

"Not good enough, doll."

I couldn't say it. I hated him right now. That's what I was thinking. This whole encounter had been planned for days. It had nothing to do with the fact that I'd acted the brat this afternoon, and everything to do with the fact that I'd staged my faux runaway scenario with Elizabeth. Jack was paying me back. Not from my script this time, but from his. And he'd known somehow that watching him give pain to someone else would be far more gut-wrenching than having to submit myself. It wouldn't have been punishment if he'd cropped me. Not true punishment. The pain would have been real, but Jack knew all about what pain did to me by now.

"I'm waiting, Sam."

"I can't, Jack." There were tears in my eyes, tears coursing down my face. "I can't watch you do that again."

He'd broken me without lifting a hand in my direction.

"I've seen you whipped. What's the difference?" There was hardness in his voice.

My dismay was caused by the way he'd touched her, the casual banter between them. The history I sensed they had, something I'd never be able to share.

"I can't—" I said again, and I turned around and put my head down. I wouldn't look at him. My whole body shook, which made the cage shake, but I didn't care. I could fall at this point, but I didn't think I would be able to feel any lower.

"Tell me what you want, Samantha."

I wouldn't look at him. I wouldn't talk to him. It would

take some doing for him to get me down, right? I could misbehave all I wanted up here in the air. Maybe I was hung from the ceiling in a birdcage, but I was momentarily out of Jack's reach.

"Two seconds," he said. "That's all it will take for the guys to be in here, for them to lower that cage to the floor. And then you'll find yourself in the same position that Juliette was in. Only you won't be asked to choose your weapon. I'll be doing the choosing for you."

Here was a threat, one that made me tighten up my thighs, squeeze them together at the vision of what he was describing. But still I refused to look at him. He could stare at the line of my back, at the curves of my ass. He could think what he would.

"Don't test me, kid."

I would not hear. I would not see. I would not speak.

"What do you want?"

What did I want?

Jack stood and walked around the cage, leaning on the wall now, staring up at me. I thought of moving once more, of facing the other way, but I couldn't make myself do it.

"Don't mess with other women," I said hoarsely. "Don't hurt them. Don't fuck them. Don't touch them."

"But men, I can torment men?"

"I don't know what you do with Alex—"

"You saw," he said.

I nodded. So this wasn't the first time they'd acted like that. I was coming in so late to this little drama. I took a deep breath. "I don't care about that." It was true, I realized as I said the words. Alex was a tool to me—I didn't know what he was to Jack. But it was the girl who had bothered me. The girl who mattered.

"Tell me what you want."

"Just you," I said, and the tears were in my words now, my voice thick. "Just you. That's all. I'll do whatever you need, Jack. But I don't want to see you play with someone else. Not like that." I wiped my eyes on my arm, feeling so brutally exposed. Nowhere to hide. I wished the cage were made of solid steel rather than bars, so Jack wouldn't be able to see me.

Jack walked away, and I heard the door open, heard him leave the room. I wondered whether I'd said the wrong thing. If I had, then it was over, wasn't it? I'd learned enough tonight to realize that I couldn't stand to watch him engage in our sort of dance with another woman. I'd rather be alone than feel this sort of pain... this shattering type of pain that had nothing to do with marks on the surface of the skin, and everything to do with marks within.

When the door opened again, I heard the heavy steps of Juliette's two hulking assistants, and in moments the cage was on the floor. Jack thanked the guys, and they left, quickly, leaving Jack to open the cage. Was he setting me free or letting me go?

I came out slowly and stood, feeling the way Alex must have, stiff from being in such a cramped and unnatural position. Jack watched me, and then he nodded. "All right," he said. But I didn't know what that meant, and I didn't move, didn't respond. "The two of us—"

"And Alex."

He shrugged, but I didn't press it.

"No other women," he continued. "I don't have a problem with that. I'm actually surprised that you did."

I continued to stare at him, and I understood that he had been trying to give me a gift. Yes, it was payback.

This intense form of discipline. But he'd thought the moving picture of him punishing another woman would have turned me on. (And he was right. I had gotten wet watching. But that didn't mean I liked it.) Yet I knew that when he saw men on me, men whipping me, the visual floored him. That Dom in the club. Alex in our bedroom. He hadn't realized I wouldn't feel the same way. Maybe I hadn't realized either.

"She's a friend," he added into my silence. "For years. She generally tops, as I'm sure you figured out. But every once in a while she needs a tune-up."

"Like Alex?"

"Alex is more complicated," Jack said, but he didn't explain any further.

I felt off balance, naked, demolished.

Jack took a step closer, and he ran his fingers through my hair. "You want me to say it, don't you? You couldn't tell by the way I act? You want me to say it."

I caught my breath. I thought I knew. But…

"Jesus, kid. I love you. Isn't that clear yet?" And the tears came steadily now. Different tears. But enough to wet my cheeks, to taste salty on my lips.

"I'm not done with you, though," Jack said, taking a final step closer. "We have unfinished business."

Chapter Sixteen:
Everybody Loves
a Happy Ending

I was eighteen the first time I heard "I love you" from a man. Brock whispered the words to me on our second date, his hand tightly gripping my hair, tipping my head back, anchoring me in place. His voice was gruff. His mouth was so close to my ear that his breath tickled my skin. I shivered all over at the tone of his voice, at the way he held me, and at the words he said. We were out on a park bench, in the dark, and I felt that anything could happen. Anything at all.

My best friend said later that Brock couldn't possibly have meant the words—not really. Not yet. How could he, when we'd known each other for fewer than forty-eight hours?

He needed to say them. And I needed to hear them. That's all that mattered.

But when Jack said he loved me, everything seemed to click into place. How brutal he'd been all night—emotionally brutal. Had he been trying to drive me off? Was this whole evening one more complicated, intricate test, by which he had tried to see if I could withstand this sort of pain, whether I would sign on for the ride or flee the chateau?

I wanted to say the words back. I wanted to say, "I love you, I love you, I love you."

Yet Jack didn't give me a chance. Unfinished business? I understood that meant I had disobeyed several times. Not leaving the room immediately upon his request when he was punishing Alex. Not turning to face him while suspended in that hateful cage. Unfinished business meant that I was going to be taking Juliette's place and Jack was going to discipline a naughty sub for the third time at the club. What stamina he had. Tireless in the face of his duty.

He moved quickly, businesslike as he surveyed the equipment in the large antique wardrobe, while I quaked inside as I watched. He'd used a crop twice this evening already. Was he in the mood for something different? I could only imagine, standing still, waiting.

Jack reached for a cane, whippet thin, mean looking as ever. Seeing it in his grip was a powerful image. Jack looked right with a cane in hand. I could easily envision him as a headmaster of yesterday, keeping his students in line. But today he had only one misbehaving pupil, one naughty schoolgirl who'd left her attire on the floor, who was stripped down and ready to accept her punishment, however cruel it might be.

"Over the horse," Jack said sternly, and I walked to the padded-leather spanking bench I'd been bound over earlier in the evening. I bent into proper position, and I waited for Jack to attach the restraints to my wrists and ankles. But he didn't.

"Hold yourself still," he said. "I don't want you to stand up. I don't want you to try and cover yourself. I don't want any movement at all." This last demand was carefully enunciated.

I don't want any movement at all.

This was more difficult than it sounded. Being bound allows the freedom to wish one could move. But forcing oneself to stay still during a whipping can feel absolutely impossible.

"Do you understand?"

"Yes, Sir."

He didn't tell me to count. He didn't give me a number, a ray of hope to shoot for. He simply stepped back and started. Unfinished business. That phrase echoed in my mind. This was only a portion of what he must have meant. If we were committed—and by his saying he loved me, I felt that we were—maybe Jack would be more open. Maybe he'd break out the old photo albums and show me what he looked like in school. Maybe he'd tell me about other girlfriends—or wives?—his past finally available for the sort of inspection that mine was to him.

Jack knew everything about me. Everything important, anyway. Jack didn't see anything shameful in my desires. Or rather, Jack loved the shame I felt for the desires. The cane slashed into me, and I sucked in my breath and held myself steady, doing my best to behave. All night long, I'd been insubordinate. Now, I would make Jack proud.

Yet my mind wouldn't quiet. I thought of one of the boys I'd dated during my freshman year in college, when I decided not to sleep with guys for a while. When I chose someone sweet, younger than I was, to hang around with. Dark curly hair. Bottle-green eyes. He sold popcorn at the theater near the school. We went out three times before he asked when we'd fuck. He'd been active earlier than most of the boys I knew—first time, in a graveyard—because he'd grown up in a small town, and there was nothing else to do.

Jack cut into me again, and I tensed and relaxed, absorbing the blow.

I'd never slept with the boy, moving right on to my lover at the grocery store, knowing that a college freshman wouldn't be able to give me what I wanted, but a thirty-four-year-old might.

My thoughts were spiraling, ricocheting, making no sense. Pain generally clears my head. But this time, I was too wound up somehow to relax. Too distracted by the fact that Jack had said he loved me....

Again the cane landed, and again, and my mind slowed down, forced by the building fire in my skin to pay attention to what was actually going on. I gripped the wood of the structure to force myself to stay put, and Jack noticed and gave me two swift blows for cheating.

"Don't hold on. I want you to keep yourself in place. Without assistance."

He spoke through gritted teeth, and I obeyed, releasing my hold, balling my hands into fists instead.

My whole body trembled in between the strikes of the cane. Jack was pacing himself, seeming to choose exactly where to land each blow, sometimes running his fingers on my skin prior to marking me with precision, right where his fingers had touched moments before.

Until he landed an unexpectedly fierce stroke, and I flinched and stood, unable to stop myself, and Jack finally had a reason to grip me up, to carry me to the table, to bind me down. He'd been waiting this whole time for me to fail. I understood that. And he seemed almost electrified as he fastened the restraints into place.

Was he going to continue with the punishment? Or...

I was dizzy with longing by now. And relief flooded through me as I watched Jack strip.

He was going to fuck me.

Oh, yes, he was going to fuck me. Although he'd taken me roughly before whipping Juliette, it felt like years since he'd been on top of me, inside of me. It felt like decades since I'd seen him whip Alex, rather than hours. And when he climbed onto the table, his hands on my body, touching me, that's when I felt myself becoming whole once more.

Chapter Seventeen:
Cherries in the Snow

Did I think that "I love you" would change everything? That the words would magically turn Jack into some tenderhearted prince? Or a docile shadow of his former Dom self?

To my delight, neither happened. Yes, he'd said he loved me. And the three little words made all the difference in our relationship. But not in the way I might have feared. Because my training by Jack intensified. He seemed more at ease leaving our gear around. There was less hiding of toys and tools. He'd leave a crop leaning against the corner in the living room for three days after he'd put it to use on my naked backside, only tossing it into the hall closet when an acquaintance from work stopped by to pick up papers.

"Can't have that," Jack winked at me, waiting for Allen to stop by. "He might think I beat you."

There were handcuffs dangling from the cold-water faucet in the tub. A paddle on the kitchen countertop.

I love you had bound me to Jack.

And it had set him free. To be who he truly was. And to be that way without any fear.

The week after our trip to the club, Jack asked me to show him what I liked. To demonstrate for him how I made myself come when he wasn't around. I hadn't known it was obvious I did this. I'd never explained to any man how I touched myself solo. Was I embarrassed? I don't know. The concept hadn't come up. Although I assumed Byron jacked off solo, because otherwise, he was more monk-like than I could believe.

"Show me," Jack insisted, "spread your legs, and show me. Or close your legs. Whatever you do. I want to see."

I hesitated. And he didn't rush me, didn't seem to think this was disobedience on my part. He was patient.

"Different ways," I said. "It's not always the same."

"Show me," Jack demanded, his voice growing more powerful. "The first way."

I stood and stripped, enjoying myself. Nervous, because I didn't know what Jack would do with the information. But excited, nevertheless. Jack followed me to the bathroom, where I adjusted the temperature with both faucets and then got into the tub. He seemed surprised when I leaned all the way back on the cold porcelain, bending my knees and sliding forward until the water from the faucet was raining down between my legs.

"Like that?" he said, eyes glowing.

I shifted my hips. "Yeah—"

"That will get you off?"

The water was already working, and I was having a difficult time speaking.

"Yeah, Jack."

"Show me."

I changed the water temperature slightly, using my feet, and Jack laughed at my dexterity.

"You want hotter or colder?"

"Depends," I said, growing breathless. "I like cold until I'm ready to come, and then gradually warmer until I get off."

I shut my eyes for a minute. This bath had the perfect water pressure, and the sensations were working through me. The water combined with the fact that Jack was watching and talking to me, turned me on even more.

Jack said, "You're close, huh?"

"Mmm-hmm."

The water stopped. Jack had turned off both faucets. "Get out and dry yourself off."

I didn't think of begging. I'd seen the look on Jack's face as he'd put the crop into the closet earlier in the evening. I knew better than to mess with him. Meekly, I climbed out of the tub and let Jack wrap one of the large black towels around my body. He watched me dry off, and then he said, "What else? Show me another trick."

I had to think for a minute, and then I hung the towel on the rack and headed down the hall. Jack followed me to our bedroom, and he seemed surprised when I went toward the hamper. I know he thought I was going to choose something from our extensive collection of toys. But I didn't want a vibrator. I wanted his T-shirt. I plucked yesterday's white one from the top of the hamper and then chose a fresh pair of panties from my drawer. I slid on the silky red bikinis then lay down on the bed.

Jack took up his position against our dresser, staring at me as I used one hand to touch myself through my panties—stroking my nether lips, circling my clit—and the other to bring Jack's shirt to my face, breathing in his scent. I was already close from the water experience.

"Why don't you touch yourself naked?"

"I always start through a barrier."

"But why?"

I thought of being a wise-ass. Of asking him which hand he jerked off with, and then querying, "But why?" Yet I was smarter than that. Not much smarter—a little smarter.

"I don't know," I told him honestly. "That's how I do it."

He settled back against the wall and watched, my fingers moving faster now, my breathing speeding up, until I could sense the climax, could almost taste how good the wave of pleasure would ultimately feel. But maybe part of me knew he wouldn't let me reach my limits. Part of me understood the torture of this game. Because I was prepared for the moment when Jack said, "Stop—" and I pulled my fingers away and looked at him.

"Now," he said, "tell me what you think about."

"What do you mean?"

"What stories are you telling yourself when you do that?"

For some reason, this was more difficult. The demonstrating had been fun, sexy. But revealing my fantasies—on demand, anyway—that was more difficult. Generally, I found myself an actor in Jack's scripts. Things happened to me, at Jack's direction. I didn't call the shots.

"Come on, Samantha…" He didn't continue, but all I had to do was think of the loving fashion he'd tucked that crop away, to know he was positively itching to use it on me this evening, if I would give him one good reason. Or maybe the word *if* wasn't right. Maybe the word was *when*.

"You know," I said, thinking fast. "All sorts of things." I'd had one experience like this before, over Nate's lap, telling him about a schoolgirl fantasy. But I sensed Jack wanted more. Jack wanted me to give him a range, to let him into the X-rated library of my mind. So that he could return there on his own, so that he could pull the fantasies off the shelves and peruse them at will.

"You're going to have to do better than that," Jack grinned. "Much better." He was moving toward me as he spoke, and I sensed he was about to bind me down, but he didn't. Instead, he sat on the bed, pushed my hands to my sides, and his fingertips took over where mine had been moments before. He stroked me through my satiny panties, his hand echoing the rotations and designs my own fingertips had been expertly creating.

"A favorite," he said. "Tell me a favorite."

"I meet you at your office," I started. "After work. Everyone's gone. I play a temp, a secretary taking the place of your regular girl. And despite everything I do, or how hard I try, I fail at all my tasks."

As I spoke, Jack slowly started to work my panties down my thighs.

"And then—" he prompted.

"Well, it's obvious, right? You have to punish me. You bend me across your desk, and you use a wooden ruler on me, when I accidentally disconnect an important phone call."

"Naughty girl."

"But the thing is," I tell him. "You've gotten the client back on the line, and he's listening on speakerphone as you stripe me with the ruler. As you make me beg and cry."

"You like that," Jack said, between my legs now, his mouth on me. "You like people hearing you, knowing that you're getting the punishment you deserve. You

101

like people knowing what you are."

"Yeah." Jack hadn't needed me to tell him how I liked a man to lick me. He was a master at this, his tongue touching me perfectly. Light enough. Hard enough. Making talking seem impossible.

"Do I fuck you in your fantasy?"

"No—that would be a reward, and I'm such a klutz at the job. Spilling coffee on your files—"

"Oh, that's worth a serious over-the-knee spanking," Jack said, his breath on me, sending me higher. "Skirt up and panties down."

"Yeah," I told him, "and then when you really need me to overnight a slew of important papers for a client, I've gone to the ladies' room to touch up my makeup."

"Is that where I find you?"

"I'm putting on my lipstick, fixing my mascara."

"And what do I do then?"

"You make me take my panties all the way off and bend me over the sink."

"And what do I do to you?"

"You have me watch my own reflection as you take off your belt and thrash me. And the sounds I make echo in the tiled room. And the tears streaking down my face embarrass me. But what's even worse is when your actual secretary comes out of the stall, having heard everything, knowing she's the queen in this environment. That I can't begin to compete."

Jack pulled back. He hadn't let me come. I'd gotten close three times now, and I was bordering on desperate.

"Is your office fantasy the same every time?"

"No, Jack. But I fuck up every time. And you punish me in different ways."

"Another one," he said. "Outside of the office."

I bit my lip, thinking. "I invite Elizabeth over to watch movies, because you've gone out of town."

"I have?"

"Mmm-hmm. And she and I are messing around. Having a slumber party for grown-up girls. Making frilly drinks. Painting each other's toenails. Watching *Gladiator*."

"That's not a chick-flick."

I shrugged.

"And then what?"

We ruin the coffee table."

"How do you do that?"

"Cherries in the Snow spills when I reach for my drink, and when I use remover to get the polish off, the chemicals wreck the wood."

"That table cost more than fifteen thousand dollars."

"I know."

"And..." He had resumed his circles now, but was moving slowly, so slowly.

"You come home then—right when I'm trying to figure out what to do—"

"I like this one," he said, "another punishment in front of an audience. But this time, it's someone you know. Someone who doesn't know anything about you. Not truly. Is that right?"

"Yes, Jack."

"And I let her watch before I send her home?"

"Yes, Jack—"

"Watch what exactly?"

"You see the color on the bottle, and you promise my ass will match that hue before you're done."

"Too bad you didn't choose a light pink. It had to be red, huh?"

"Yes, Jack."

"Sweet," Jack said, and I could tell he wasn't messing with me, because he sat up then, stripped quickly, and flipped me on the bed. In seconds, he was inside of me, fucking me, knowing exactly how prepped I was by all that foreplay.

"And now?" he said. "What are you thinking of now?"

"I don't—" I panted. "I don't tell stories while we fuck."

"But what do you think about?"

"What you might do to me next."

He slapped my ass hard. "Like that?"

"Yes, Sir."

And again, in rhythm now to the way he was fucking me. I felt transported by having been on the edge for so long, and when Jack pressed against me, running one hand over my pussy, pinching my clit between his finger and thumb, I came in a series of glittering waves.

"I think we *will* plan a slumber party," he said, pressing his face against my neck as he gripped my hips. I could tell he was close. "But I think we'll invite Alex, instead."

And then he was coming, holding me tight and coming hard. Coming to the fantasies in my own head. Fantasies that blended and melded with his own.

Chapter Eighteen:
Would I Lie to You?

"I'll be home at lunch," Jack said over the phone.

"Do you want me to order in?"

"No."

"Do you want me to make reservations?"

"No."

"Do you want—"

"You," he said. "I want you."

I thought of him at his desk making the call. Visualized him surrounded by the chaos of his work life, the clients, the phone calls, the constant stress. And then I thought of him taking a step back from his world and into ours, pausing long enough to call me.

"How?" I asked, understanding there was more to come. That he would give instructions as to exactly how he wanted me.

"In high heels," Jack said, "the black patent-leather ones."

"Yes, Jack."

"And the ruffled white panties. You know the ones."

I did. They were his favorite of all of my knickers. I waited to hear what else. What skirt to put on. Or what kinky uniform. But he said, "I'll only have a little while. And this is what I want—I want to come in and find you ready, standing by the chair, waiting. I'm going to sit down, and you are to bend over my lap. Immediately. I'm in a generous mood today, kid. You choose the paddle. Have it ready for me. Because all I can think of doing right now is spanking your luscious ass. That image is what's keeping me from getting any work done at all."

I listened carefully.

"I've got a million things to get through before seven," Jack explained, "and you're not letting me. I'm sitting here at my desk with a hard-on, wishing I could bend you over my lap right here and spank the daylights out of you."

I squeezed my thighs together, feeling the wetness start.

"So instead, I'm going to have to cancel an important lunch, and break every law of physics to get home and then back to work by my first afternoon meeting. And because I have to do that, you're going to have to pay."

He could almost make me come if he kept talking to me like that.

"So go choose, Sam," Jack murmured. "Go choose the paddle, and get ready like I asked. I'll be home in less than an hour."

He disconnected the call before I said, "Yes, Sir," but I whispered the words anyway, even though I knew he couldn't hear them. I'd been writing, but I was at a good stopping place. And there was no way I could go back to work now. Not with images of an impending spanking swirling in my head. I walked quickly to the bedroom, stripping off my clothes on the way, my shirt over my head, my bra next. I pulled off my jeans and panties once I was in the room, and then searched the top dresser drawer for the ruffled knickers Jack had requested—only to discover they were nowhere in sight.

I'd been turned on since I'd first heard his voice on the phone. Now, I was nervous. Jack had been specific. He hadn't told me to select any old pair. He'd wanted these, a gift he'd given me himself. I rummaged through the hamper, but didn't find them there, either.

What the fuck? Panties don't walk away on their own.

I kept on the black set that I had, and chose a paddle quickly. One that I knew would make Jack smile. The SLUT paddle would imprint the word into my fair skin if he spanked me hard enough. I put on the shoes, spiked heels that I'd finally learned to walk in. And then I searched the whole place for my missing undies.

White. Maybe they'd gotten mixed in with the sheets. I tore through the linen closet, but came up empty handed. Next thought—I'd put them with the dry cleaning. I emptied the canvas sack, searching through my rumpled dresses and several of Jack's sweaters. But no luck. When I heard the key in the lock, I looked around the room in distress. I'd managed to trash the place in my search, and I was going to fail. If I'd had a tail, it would have hung forlornly between my legs as I made my way to the living room. When Jack opened the door, I was standing by the chair, as he'd commanded, but I could tell from the look on his face that he wasn't pleased.

"I only asked you to do three things," Jack said.

"I know, Jack, but—"

He held up a finger. "I hear excuses all day long," he said. "One after another after another. I don't need to hear yours."

I wanted to keep talking, but his expression froze me solid.

Jack didn't sit in the chair. He didn't beckon me forward. He simply stared at me, disappointment in his eyes, until I lowered my head, desolate. Desperate.

"Take them off," he said, and I worked quickly, slipping the black satin panties down my thighs and stepping gingerly out of them. "Forget the paddle," he said, "Go on back to the bedroom."

My heart sank. I'd been hoping to clean up the wreck of the room after he'd gone back to work, leaving him none the wiser about my useless search.

When Jack walked into his normally sterile bedroom, he shook his head.

"Three simple things," he said flatly. "That's all. I had a bitch of a morning, and I wanted to come home and play with you. Take an hour off. And this is what I find." He gestured at the rumpled sheets, the emptied hamper, the colorful spill of dry cleaning on the hardwood floor like paint tipped on a canvas.

"Get on the bed."

I hurried to obey as Jack removed his coat and tossed it to the chair.

"Face up, arms over your head."

Quickly, I did as he said, closing my eyes as he clicked the cuffs on my wrists, as he bound my ankles so that my legs were spread wide apart. He'd ignored my choice of the SLUT paddle, and now opened the cabinet, pulling out his favorite flogger. I winced before he'd even started, anticipating the pain. But even having been whipped like this before—the first shock of the tiny strands against my tender skin was unexpected. Jack worked me mercilessly with crisscrossing strokes, and I arched my body uselessly,

108

my brain confused by the mixed signals of the toy. Jack was hurting me, but making me wetter with every stroke. I wanted more—but how could I want more? Being punished like this was one of the most difficult experiences for me to accept.

Yet I could tell that Jack relished every moment.

For days now, I'd felt that Jack was on a mission. He wanted to climb inside of me, to know where I went when I got quiet. To understand all aspects of the way my mind worked. It was unnerving, yet flattering. I'd spent such a long time trying to make Byron happy, completely subjugating myself, stamping down my own desires, that I was put off guard having someone so dedicated to searching out what gave me pleasure.

And not only what—but why.

It wasn't enough for Jack to know that I got even more turned on if I had to anticipate a spanking for several hours before receiving one. He methodically figured out exactly how far to take it.

"You're wet," he said, pausing to run his fingers down the split of my nether lips. "So fucking wet, naughty girl. There's no real way to punish you, is there? It all gets you off, my little pain slut."

As he spoke, he undid the bindings on my ankles, turning me face down now, and I could only guess what he had in mind. No mere paddling. No... I turned to look as he chose his toy, and the word escaped from my lips before I could stop myself. "No..."

"What did you say?"

"Sir," I said, knowing I wasn't fooling him. But he was holding a paddle I'd never even touched before. An oversized wood fraternity-style paddle, black lacquered, drilled through with holes.

"Did you say 'no'?"

I shook my head.

"Are you lying now?"

Oh fuck… Why hadn't I been able to find the panties? If I had, he would have used the SLUT paddle on me, and then he'd probably have fucked me bent over the chair before returning to work. Now, he was going to try out a new toy, and I would end up standing for the rest of the day.

"Yes, Jack. Sorry, Jack." *What do I need to say, Jack, to make you put that thing back?*

"Up," he demanded. I want your ass up, as if it's begging for each stroke."

I raised my hips into the position, and then tensed, waiting. Waiting…

Jack smacked the paddle against my ass, and I cried out from the immediate pain. Being spanked in the middle of the day, with unexpected force, somehow made the whole situation harder to deal with. I don't know why, like I don't know why sometimes the crop made me cry and beg, and other times I could hold myself still and take it. Pain is variable rather than consistent. Everything matters. The circumstances. The outfits. The tension.

Jack gave me a good, hearty punishment with his choice of tools, before dropping the frat paddle on the mattress and undoing the cuffs on my wrists. I could tell from the look in his eyes that he had no plans to fuck me right now.

"You wait here," he said, and I heard him return to the cabinet once more. When he was back at my side, I felt the familiar swipe of lube between my cheeks, and then Jack slid in one of the larger plugs, making me wince at his lack of gentleness.

"You'll wear that until I get home, and then we'll finish."

"Yes, Jack." I stood carefully, and when he gave me permission, I got dressed. Not in jeans, but in my favorite soft tie-pants and a white T-shirt. I padded barefoot down the hall to say good-bye to him, and I could hear him making a call from the kitchen phone.

I stayed meekly in the living room, not wanting to disturb him, to get into any more trouble. My gaze happened to wander to the outer pocket of his briefcase, where a hint of white lace could be seen.

Chapter Nineteen:
Pictures of You

When I woke up one morning, there was a Polaroid on my pillow. A Polaroid Jack must have taken before he left. It was still early in the morning—earlier than he usually headed out to his office—but he was in the middle of a huge case at work, and for several weeks, he'd told me, his hours were going to be haywire. Late in the evening. Early in the morning.

Jack never seemed to need as much sleep as normal humans. But I guess I'm a bit like that myself. When I hear people talk about their standard eight hours, or even their necessary six hours, I am in awe. I tend to sleep hard for about two to three hours at a time, and I often wake up and work in between.

Yet even though Jack was busy, focused, he found time for me. Or rather, he made time for me. He left trinkets in places where he knew I'd discover them. Surprises to excite me or turn me on—a new paddle hanging from the back of the bathroom door. An expensive set of heavy metal cuffs in the drawer with the silverware. And today—a photo. *This* photo. It was of his leather belt, coiled neatly, almost snake-like.

I looked at the picture, ran my fingers lightly over the surface. It was dry. He'd been gone for a bit, then. I headed down the hallway to the coffeemaker, poured myself a cup, and located the second photo waiting for me on the countertop. I was reminded of a story told to me by my friend Angelo. His new girlfriend had delighted him one evening with votive candles leading from the front door to his bedroom. Rose petals everywhere. Champagne poured and ready. She was waiting in a dainty sort of nightgown, and he had been floored by the preparation work all done for him. He told this story over breakfast, with her present, and several of his foreign friends around, who needed the story translated into Italian and French. I watched the girl, saw her face flush, and knew she'd never thought he'd share their private moments over eggs Benedict. But the care she'd taken had overwhelmed him—the idea that someone would do all of that for him—and he'd needed to share.

The second photo was of a schoolgirl skirt Jack had bought for me. Red-and-black plaid, almost decent in length. He'd taken the picture with the skirt hanging from the door of the closet. I wondered if he'd shot these photos that morning, or if this was an idea he'd had for some time. I brought my coffee back to the bedroom and snagged the skirt from the closet. Sharing the same hanger was a white T-shirt and black cashmere cardigan, and attached to one of the clips on the hanger was Polaroid number three: a pair of knee-length leather boots with chrome buckles on the sides. Jack loved it when I wore hardcore boots with girly skirts. I grabbed the boots from the floor of the

113

closet, turning them upside down, into the game now.

Out fell the next clue: a picture of the fishnet stockings and panties he obviously wanted me to wear. I hurried to my top dresser drawer, in a flush now, aroused by the game. As I said, Jack had been busy. Not too busy to fuck me, of course. Or to play our kinky little games. But focused on work. I could tell. He'd stay up even later than usual, and when he was at my side in the bed, I knew he didn't fall asleep right away. He thought things over, processed them. I hated to disturb him when he was like that, and I'd fall asleep half the bed away, lonely even so close to him.

But this was different. Jack had planned this. Had taken the time to go through all of these steps, setting my morning routine on its head. Setting my day into completely unexpected motion.

In the dresser drawer was the next photo. And when I saw it, I felt my breath catch. It was a storefront in West Hollywood. One that I recognized immediately, but I hadn't been to before: a high-end piercing boutique.

I stopped in place, holding the photo and wanting to call Jack. Everything I'd done so far was automatic, following commands he hadn't even given me verbally. Wasn't I well trained? But this was different. He knew my history, knew that I'd had one of my tattoos done for Connor. I'd been waiting, I think, for him to come up with his own way to top that experience.

Was this what Jack had in mind?

Jack didn't have any piercings of his own. I couldn't imagine him with pierced ears or nipples, or pierced anything... I'd dated men who had rings in different locations, silver hoops that suited them. But none of that would have worked for Jack. So the trip to the studio was going to be all about me. And what did that mean?

What part of me was to be adorned?

I sat down on the bed, still in my white drawstring pants and the skimpy tee I'd slept in. Slowly, I drank my coffee, letting the java work its magic. Letting the hot bitter liquid wake me up. I had a feeling that this was the last photo. And so what did that mean? I spread the pictures out on the bed. I'd assumed I had found them all in proper order.

Number one, the belt—was that a threat?

Follow the commands, or this is what you'll get.

Or was it a reward?

Do this for me, and I'll tan your sweet hide.

Either could be the case, and both scenarios turned me on equally. I shuffled the photos, like a tarot reader I'd been to once in New Orleans, wondering if mixing up the order would help. But no. There was the outfit to wear, the place to go. So what did the belt have to do with the rest? He couldn't possibly want me to put it on.

I said fuck it and headed down the hall to take a shower.

When I returned to the bedroom, everything seemed clearer. I'd get dressed in Jack's chosen outfit, search the place for any missing clues, and if I couldn't find any, I'd go to the piercing studio and wait. That made sense to me.

Once I had on the modified schoolgirl uniform—no self-respecting actual schoolgirl would have chosen the kick-ass motorcycle boots—I grabbed up the pictures and started down the hall. Then stopped.

I was supposed to bring the belt. That made sense. I went back to Jack's closet and searched through his collection until I found the one he'd photographed. When I pulled it from the rack, I saw another picture clipped to the tail of the leather.

The final picture was of Alex. Posed with sunglasses tilted down so I could see his eyes. A mocking smile on his face. As if he knew his mug was the last thing I expected to find.

How did Jack know me so well? How had he known that I wouldn't grab the belt first, that I wouldn't locate the pictures out of order? I looked at them again, and this time, flipping them over, I saw tiny numbers written in the bottom right-hand corners. The belt was number one, Alex was number six. But what was I supposed to do with the photo of Alex? Did the picture mean I was supposed to call him?

Precisely as I thought that, I heard the front door open. What timing. And Alex called out, "You ready?"

"Yes, Alex."

"You have the belt?"

I headed toward the living room, the leather in my hands. "Yes, Alex."

"Good girl," he grinned at me, enjoying himself as always. "Now assume the position."

Chapter Twenty:
Take This Longing

I did. He wouldn't give a command more than twice. And although I'm a curious little kitty, I wasn't anxious to find out what would happen if I tested this rule. That was something I'd save for a different day, a day when I craved attention.

Quickly, I handed over Jack's belt and then turned around and bent forward, hands on my ankles. I knew exactly how he liked me, and I would show him obedience right now. As one more effort to apologize for the intricate trick I'd played on him. Besides, I was starting to understand the depth of his connection with Jack. I knew my life would be far easier if Alex were an ally rather than an enemy. At the moment, we seemed to be at a neutral ground. He no longer seemed as angry as he had at first, yet we weren't back to being friends. If we'd ever been friends.

He flipped my little plaid skirt up in the rear and then stood back from me. I could easily visualize him in my head, doubling the belt, deciding where to strike, how hard to start. I wondered why Jack wanted me thrashed, especially since I had done everything according to the photos—at least I thought I had, anyway. Had Alex seen something amiss in my outfit? Was there a photo clue I hadn't found? One that would have explained another step in the morning's procedure? After two blows, Alex answered my unspoken question.

"This was for me," he said. "Jack said to use my discretion. I could punish you or not, according to my whims." The pain was muted by my panties, but the leather stung nonetheless. "And you look so hungry when you're holding a belt in your hands. It's hard to refuse that image."

Did I? Was I like some adult, female version of Oliver? Holding out a belt instead of a bowl? *Please, Sir, may I have another?* Perhaps, but no matter what, I was never calling Alex "Sir."

"Count them out for me," Alex said, and I felt his fingers sliding my panties down my thighs. He'd given me the first few as a mere warm-up. Now, he was going to punish me for real—leather on skin. I hoped he couldn't tell that I was growing aroused.

Alex struck me hard and quick, so quick that I had a difficult time keeping up with the counting, which gave him a reason to add several strokes at the end. The leather landed louder on my naked skin than it had over the fabric of my panties, and even the sound managed to turn me on. I wished Jack were punishing me instead of Alex, but I couldn't hide from myself the fact that I had been jonesing for some sort of relief—or release—since I'd found the initial photograph.

Yet as he cut into me, I knew he wasn't using the belt on

my hide for my pleasure. He was doing it for his. Because clearly, Alex wasn't going to forgive me for my indiscretion. I don't know what upset him more. The fact that I'd asked him to lie for me. Or the fact that I'd tricked Jack with Elizabeth, playing a game to make Jack worry. But I also didn't know what type of girl Alex thought I should be. Did he really think Jack wanted someone perfect? Someone who never pressed boundaries, who never put up a fight? How fun would it be for a Dom to punish some docile meek mouse? (And after being a docile, meek mouse for years with Byron, I wasn't going to let that happen again.)

Still, when Alex dropped the belt, I understood that he had decided not to work me too severely—which was a bit of a worry. Was he leaving the big job for Jack? Whatever his reason, he gave me more than twenty good strokes, then flipped my skirt back down and told me to stand.

"You know where we're going?"

"Yeah."

"And why?"

Now, I shook my head.

"But you could guess."

"It's a piercing studio. I'm not an idiot."

Alex gave me a look that seemed to say, "We'll see."

Alex drove me to the piercing boutique, but he didn't walk up the stairs with me. I left the car and headed in on my own, and when I opened the door to the studio, there was Jack. Waiting. Ready.

I remembered a Howard Stern show I'd seen, in which this gorgeous goth girl had told the world that when she'd gotten her clit pierced she'd come like a jackhammer. The sound bite was forever in my head, but I didn't want to experience that myself. Somehow, tattoos are easier for me than piercings. That doesn't make any sense, I know. Tattoos are far more permanent.

Jack was in a discussion with one of the employees, and I saw him gesture to a jewelry display close by. Then he came toward me and put his arms around me. "You liked the game?"

"Yes, Jack."

"And you found all the clues?"

I nodded.

He flipped me around without warning, lifted my skirt, and then slid my panties down slightly. I flushed instantly cherry, knowing that the man he'd been talking to now had a clear view of my ass.

"Then why did Alex have to whip you?"

"He didn't have to. He just did."

Jack laughed, a low sound that told me he understood exactly what I meant, and that he'd known from the start that Alex wouldn't let an opportunity like that go by.

"Go choose," he said next, pointing to the same display he'd been perusing with the employee. "Show me what you like."

But when I went over to look at the rings, I felt dizzy. I didn't want to do this. Yes, I thought piercings were sexy. I'd loved running my tongue over the ones on a former beau's chest. But I didn't want any for myself. And I wondered how I might explain that to Jack. Explain in a way that didn't make him think I was being stubborn for no reason.

The clerk was busy showcasing the various ring sizes, when I turned around to look at Jack, now talking to a pretty, multi-pierced multi-tattooed chicklet, another employee.

"Jack—"

He came to my side, but not in a hurry. He thought I'd found something I liked.

"I don't think I can do this."

"It's not that painful," the clerk assured me, and Jack laughed again, knowing that the concept of how much it might (or might not) hurt wasn't what was bothering me.

Kindly, Jack took me to a corner of the store. "What's the problem?" he asked, and I could see his mind working. He'd taken off work somehow in this crazy-busy week, and he'd set this scenario up to thrill me. And I was balking at the gift. I could see more than that. Jack liked the idea of me lifting my shirt, revealing my breasts to a stranger who would—simply through the nature of the business—cause me pain. He wanted to see me wince or bite my lip. He wanted to see me squirm. And later, after I'd healed, Jack was going to pull on those hoops with his teeth, tug on them, torment me in a brand-new way. And even if all of that sounded delightful to me, I couldn't do it.

"I don't want to."

He stared at me for a moment, as if trying to see inside of me. How crazy is it that I would have pointed to a design on the wall at Sunset Strip Tattoo in a heartbeat. That I would have revealed whatever body part Jack craved, that I would have taken the pain as I had in the past, as if it were nothing. (I know that people have totally different thresholds. I took Elizabeth for her first tattoo. She wanted a cross with rosary beads on her ankle, and she had this idea of filling the cross in to look like stained glass. But after the mere outline of the design, she stopped, unable to continue. I've had tattoos done on that same area, and it's not as if I didn't feel a thing, but I didn't feel on the verge of passing out, as Liz did.)

"You don't want—"

"I don't want to be pierced."

He didn't even hesitate. He simply said thank you to the employees and led me down the stairs. There was no anger in his face, no pressure to "do it for him." Alex seemed surprised to see us back so early, but Jack didn't say a word to him. He gave me a kiss, warm and sweet, and then pulled an envelope from his pocket. "I have to get back to work," he said. "I'll meet you later. Alex will tell me which one you choose."

When I got back into the car, I opened the envelope. There were three more Polaroids inside.

The game continued...

Chapter Twenty-One:
This Is the Picture

Jack wasn't angry. I could tell. The request at the piercing parlor was not the sort of command for which he expected obedience. Submitting to piercing was far different from being told to bend over for a spanking. Or to lift my skirt to show him the marks Alex had left. Or to drop to my knees and part my lips.

And yet...

Alex was smirking, as if he had known from the start that I wouldn't be able to go through with the whole thing. His expression made me feel uneasy. I was fairly sure he'd seen the pictures in the envelope, but I didn't hand them over right away, didn't show him what I was looking at. I wanted to tell him to go fuck himself, which he must have guessed, because he slowly unbuttoned the front of his neatly pressed ocean-blue dress shirt, showing me his pierced nipples.

Had he sported the rings in at the club? Or were they new? And if they were new, had Jack gone with him to watch him get pierced? Jealousy flamed through me. Was Jack branding both of his slaves? The thought twisted my stomach, and although I was fairly sure that if I asked, Alex would share the information I craved, I refused to give him the chance.

His smile broadened. He actually winked at me before buttoning the shirt back up.

The urge to fight with him grew stronger, but Alex still had Jack's belt with him, and I had the feeling that if I fought with him, he'd use it.

Instead, I did my best to ignore him entirely—as if I were all alone in the car—and I shuffled the pictures over and over, trying to figure out what to do. What to choose. Trying to understand what the photos meant.

Photo number one was of a famous sex toy store up on Sunset. If I picked that one, did that mean I had to select something in the store? Something for me to wear, or something for Jack to use on me?

The second picture was of the salon where I'd worked for a very short time before moving in with Jack.

The final picture was of a restaurant.

None of the photos seemed to go together. And none of them seemed to match the concept of piercing in the slightest. I had thought that if I didn't go through with the first choice, there would be similar options—somewhat similar, anyway. A tattoo was the first thing that came to mind. But what was Jack offering instead? A shopping spree? A haircut? A meal?

"You can go to the store first, or hit the salon. It's up to you," Alex said, evenly. Clearly, he knew exactly what I held in my hands.

"What am I supposed to do at the salon?"

"You'll see, won't you?"

"You're a lot of help," I snarled, unable to stop myself. Alex wasn't making this day any easier.

My mood didn't appear to affect his at all. He gave me a winning smile, then touched Jack's belt. "Watch yourself. I've got carte blanche today," he said.

"And what's that supposed to mean?"

"Give me a reason," he said, "any reason at all." His smile had clicked off. "Because you know what, little girl? I'm dying to take you out of the car, bend you over the hood, and whip you right here." His voice took on an even more menacing tone. "And you know Jack's going to be checking later, checking to see exactly how you misbehaved. I've had enough of your attitude for today. Don't test my patience any longer."

I sat quietly after that, understanding that Alex could do what he said even if I were on my very best behavior, but deciding not to give him a reason.

"So you've chosen?" Alex said, glaring at me.

"Yes, Alex. I'll go to the salon."

I wondered as I walked up the stairs whether this would have been the natural progression of events had I gone through with the piercing. Was a haircut always on the books for me? Or would this have been cancelled had I done what Jack requested? I probably would never find out, I decided, as I presented myself at the desk. Jack must have booked one stylist all day long in order to have him open when I showed up. I knew the expense of that sort of whim, and I felt awed as one of my former coworkers led me to Matteo's station. He was one of the most elite in the building.

"Jack's made a request," Matteo told me, and he had the same look on his face that Alex had. A look I took to mean that he knew something I didn't.

"Yes?"

"And he wants me to cut you with your back to the mirror."

I looked into his eyes. That meant I wouldn't know the results until Matteo was finished. I'd have the whole duration of the cut to imagine what was happening. But this was different from being pierced. No matter what—hair grows back. Did I trust Jack? That was the real question.

"Fine," I said, and Matteo's expression changed slightly. He seemed impressed that I hadn't asked any additional questions, hadn't tried to get him to tell me what was going to happen.

After being shampooed, I was back in the chair, facing Matteo, who paid no attention to me at all while he worked. He was intent, but I could tell that my hair was changing drastically simply by the amount that fell to the floor around me. He didn't spin me around until after the blow-dry, and what I saw was almost surreal. I'd come into the salon with hair that reached between my shoulder blades. Now, I had a bob, sleek and chic, yes, but about nine inches shorter. I closed my eyes for a moment then opened them again, slowly.

"Do you like it?" Matteo asked, ruffling my hair with his hand, looking at me with a critical eye—not seeing me, only my hair.

I nodded. "Yes." It was one of those moments of enlightenment, when I realized exactly how well Jack knew me. He had chosen this cut for me, and it worked. I looked like a different person, sophisticated, yet sexy.

Matteo kissed me on both cheeks and then swept the draped cloth off my shoulders, releasing me.

Back in the car, I couldn't stop touching my hair,

running my fingers up the back of my neck. I felt so much more exposed without the curtain of hair I was used to. Alex still had that smile on his face, and finally I said, "What?"

"If you'd refused, Jack told me to use this," he said, and he popped open the glove box, revealing the type of razor men use to shave their heads.

I shuddered but didn't say a word.

It was time for the next stop.

Chapter Twenty-Two:
Carte Blanche

I wasn't a virgin. Not to this location, anyway. I'd been to this sex toy store before, on a first date with a guy during the summer Byron and I went out but before we were exclusive. It had been for a laugh then, both of us pointing at the different devices (penile pumps and pocket pussies) and giggling helplessly. And although we'd made out in the man's car, we hadn't bought anything. Perhaps it wasn't the best first-date location.

But shopping there with Alex was something else. As might have been expected, he spent most of the time admiring the displays of punishment devices: paddles, floggers, slappers, crops, and canes. When I tried to get him to tell me what I was supposed to do in the place, he said lightly, "Bend over and let me try this one out."

"Come on, Alex. What does Jack want?" I tried my best to be flirtatious, but Alex didn't fall for my friendly act.

"He wants you to be smart enough to figure it out for

yourself." He waved a mean-looking implement called a prison strap in the air. "Now bend over."

There were a few customers in the store on this weekday afternoon—some girls in a corner buying for a bachelorette party, I guessed. Alex's eyes said to obey, and I offered my rear to him, bending over only slightly. He didn't think much of that. He pushed me forward firmly, so that I had to catch the edge of the nearest table to keep my balance, flicked up my skirt with the tip of the device, and then slapped the weapon hard against my seat. And although I flushed instantly, I had a feeling the clerk had seen worse than this. Nobody said a thing to us, and Alex happily placed his purchase on the counter before returning to peruse the rest of the wares.

But what about me? What was I supposed to do? The photo simply showed the exterior of the building. There had been no other clues.

When I walked past a mirror on the wall, I caught my reflection and stopped. The new haircut was divine. I knew that. Striking enough to make me want to look over and over. Matteo's expertise had actually transformed me. I looked like a different person. This had happened to me once before. When I got to college, I was supremely shy. I'd had an unforgettable summer vacation—and several summer romances—in Europe, but being back again with my peers cowed me. I've never been able to blend easily with people my own age, and I wound up falling back into my earlier bad habits—wearing skinny blue jeans and oversized bowling shirts and oxfords. Letting my hair fall into my eyes. Forgoing makeup. Hiding.

Until one afternoon when three bored sorority girls on my floor decided to do a makeover for me. It was more than halfway through the school year when they blow-dried my hair, getting it out of my eyes for once. They added the lightest wash of cosmetics, chocolate eyeliner, a few coats of mascara, and pale berry lipstick. And then one poured me into her tightest little black dress and paraded me around the floor.

And none of the boys recognized me.

I'd been their neighbor for months, had eaten in the dining hall with them, attended classes with them, hung out in their rooms while they got drunk. I'm not making this up. They thought I was a different girl.

That's what I looked like now. A different girl.

And I understood. Jack wanted me to dress myself. To come up with some new outfit. To surprise him at the restaurant he'd chosen.

I returned to the part of the store filled with assorted clothes generally found on strippers or lingerie models. But in and around the feather-trimmed nighties and lace-edged boyshorts were several wearable-in-real-life pieces. While Alex was lost in his world of pain among the canes and the crops, I grabbed several dresses, slacks, and skirts and headed to the tiny room in the back, behind the leopard-print curtain, to try on my choices.

Everything looked unpredictable on me now. The new hair had changed my whole attitude. It wasn't that I'd never be able to pull off a schoolgirl look again, but this style made me want to rock black leather slacks, a hard-as-nails studded belt, and a tight-fitted, long-sleeved T-shirt. My boots worked perfectly with the rest of the attire, and I wore the outfit up the stairs to get Alex's opinion.

He had placed two more items next to the register: a crop and a quirt. And he had that impish look on his face again.

"What do you think?" I managed to ask, turning

around. The giggling girls buying dildos for their soon-to-be-married friend turned to look, as well.

"You figured out the goal, then?" he asked back, apparently unimpressed with how long I'd taken.

I shrugged. "One more thing." I snagged a wallet from below the register, complete with a silver wallet chain, and I added this to my outfit. In the mirror, I looked tough. Joan Jett tough. And I liked it.

Alex paid for all purchases, laughing when the clerk offered to wrap his items in brown paper. "No need," he said magnanimously. "I'll be using them soon."

He walked me out of the store with his hands full of a pain-tinged bouquet, and a bit of my inner swagger wore off when he made me hold the devices in my lap while he drove.

"Jack's meeting you for dinner in Santa Monica," he said. "But we have a few hours to kill first."

Absentmindedly, I found myself fingering the leather prison strap he'd chosen first. I could still feel the echo of pain from that one solitary blow. I watched as Alex drove us easily through the city, understanding he had a plan when I realized he was heading away from the beach, toward Griffith Park instead.

"Jack wanted me to prep you," he said, his voice low, and I realized his mood was changing as we grew closer to whatever destination he had in mind. "Prep you for tonight's activities. And he said to use my best judgment on how to do that."

Jack had given me to Alex for the afternoon. I understood that. And I felt nervous as Alex parked the car and walked to my side, opening the door for me like a gentleman would. But he was no gentleman. He could never be what Jack was. He could try. But he always seemed to be acting. The moves didn't come naturally.

"A little walk," he said, "to a secluded spot. Where it won't matter if you make noise."

I looked at him, not obeying right away, trying to gauge exactly what he had planned.

"Don't test me, little girl"—his pet phrase for the day—"I'm still in a good mood."

I followed him out of the car and down the path he'd chosen, walking in gear that was clearly ridiculous for a hike in the park. But Alex didn't take me far. He had a location in mind, secluded as he'd promised, yet he surprised me once more when we'd reached the destination. Rather than having me assume his chosen position—whatever that might be, bent over to touch my toes, or straight up, leaning against a tree—he gripped me in his embrace. Tight. And then he backed away, slightly, looking down at me. For a moment, I thought he would slap my face. And then I thought he would kiss me.

"Do you love Jack?"

The question caught me even more off guard.

"Yes. Of course."

"Really? You really love him?"

"Yes, Alex."

And then, more strange than anything, more unexpected than everything, "Could you love me, too?"

Chapter Twenty-Three:
Love

"Could you, Samantha?"

I am a deeply monogamous person.

Oh, yeah, right, I can hear you saying snidely. *You cheated, like, three times on your fiancé. Not three times, actually. But with three different lovers. You had several ménages. You kissed that waiter. You were willingly whipped by Jack's assistant....*

But I didn't love any of those people. That's the difference. So, yes, I'll admit it's pathetic I didn't love the man I was supposed to marry. I understand that. And it's downright cruel that I took pleasure in bending over for Connor while wearing Byron's diamond and ruby ring. Yet none of that changed my fundamental feeling—love should be between two people. That once I found the type of love I craved, it's all I would want.

I'd been there before—with Brock. And yeah, Brock was a criminal. A thief and a drug dealer. And yeah, none of that fucking mattered. I loved him. With that kind of love you read about, that unreal passion that makes everything—and everyone else—fade away. I knew what that emotion was like when I was eighteen. Some people die without ever finding it, poor souls, and before Jack, I thought I'd never find that sort of love again.

So Alex's query threw me into a spin.

Was he asking me this as a test from Jack? With Jack, you never knew.

Was he trying to get me back for wanting him to lie? That seemed far-fetched. My request had been minor. This was huge.

He came a step closer, and I took a step back. He didn't frighten me. I don't know why. We were out in the woods together, and he had weapons of a sort with him. And yet he seemed vulnerable, and I felt as if for the first time with Alex, I had the upper hand.

"Why are you asking me that?"

"I need to know."

Jack and I weren't married. And he definitely had an interest in seeing me with other people. He'd already incorporated Alex into our world physically. So what was the difference? Or, rather, what was the problem?

Perhaps Alex was tired of being a tool. Or maybe before I came along, he was the one sitting at Jack's side in the passenger seat. But I didn't think so. Somehow, I guessed that Alex had always been relegated to assistant. To helper.

"I don't know," I said, my mind flickering to a paper I wrote back in school. We'd been assigned to write about *King Lear,* and my composition was called "Lear in Love." I followed that emotion through the play, and I inserted famous quotes about love in my essay. (I got an A+, I'll say.) But when I look back now, I realize I've been obsessed with the concept of love for years. I thought I knew what it meant.

And yet, when Alex asked me his question, the whole concept of love changed in my mind. Could I love him? That's what he wanted to know. I'd never been in this situation before.

Brock said he loved me on day two. The feeling was more than mutual. We were so well suited for each other. I'll never in my life know how he found me. How he saw me. How he knew. But I will always believe in love at first sight based on that experience.

Byron said he loved me after he thought someone else wanted me more. I returned the statement, knowing I didn't feel the same way about him as I had about Brock, but thinking maybe you only get one shot at that sort of powerful body-thrilling love in your life.

Jack said he loved me when I needed to know. When I couldn't stand not knowing anymore.

And Alex?

My world felt turned upside down.

"Could you someday?" His voice was soft. His eyes were cast down. I had hated him. I had seen the pleasure he'd taken in giving me pain. I had witnessed how much my embarrassment thrilled him. And yet sometimes I'd felt almost as if he were a brother, that strong pull of sibling rivalry alive and well in our mutual quest to please Jack. But did any of those things mean I couldn't...I didn't...

He was silent. He was waiting. I looked at him as if seeing him for the first time. Alex was younger than Jack—and I do tend to like my men a bit older. But he was older than me, old enough. He liked what I liked. That was clear. If there had been no Jack in the picture, would I have fallen for him? For his coldness. For the way he was methodical in all of his dealings—from the style in which he dressed to his extreme punctuality.

Fuck, I didn't know.

I loved Jack. That was clear in my head. But I didn't know what to say. I sat down.

Can you choose who you love?

Alex stayed standing, and I looked up at him. "I don't know," I said again. "I'm sorry."

He smiled, kind of shyly. "That's not a no," he said.

I shrugged. "You confused me."

He sat down now. Not close enough to touch me, but nearby. "I've been wondering for a while," he said.

What would it mean? Would I have two Dominant men in my life? I already did. What would the difference be if I started to look at Alex as anything other than a human device, a useful tool controlled by Jack?

"You love him, though," I said.

"Yes."

And that one word made my heart ache. Fundamentally, truly, deep down in my core, I am so very wired to be a one-woman man. And I can hear you saying, *Ha! Right.* But I am. If I'd met Brock later, when I was older. If he hadn't been arrested. If I hadn't gone off to school.

If... If... If...

I wish I could tie this up nicely. I wish I could say we came to some sort of agreement out there in the wilderness in the middle of Los Angeles. But all I can say is that Alex smiled at me. That he cocked his head and looked me over. And then he said, "I'm a hypocrite."

"What do you mean?"

"I'm going to ask you what you asked me."

I stared at him.

"I'm going to beg you, even," he continued.

He didn't want me to tell Jack. He was asking me to lie for him. The weapons were still at his side. The crop and the prison strap and the rest. He gathered them up and handed them over.

"Whatever you want," he said. "Do it. But don't tell Jack..."

Chapter Twenty-Four:
Liar

I never lied to Brock.

There are a million reasons why I was always honest with him, but the simplest is that he would have known if I hadn't been. He would have looked into my dark brown eyes and been able to tell in a split second that I wasn't being truthful. Of course, he didn't maintain the same level of honesty with me. He told me he was in the import/export business rather than admitting he dealt drugs to the upper echelon of Silicon Valley. He said he was out of town when he was in jail.

Ultimately I didn't care. He didn't lie to me about things that meant anything. His mouth on my neck was all that mattered. His body pressed up against mine in the alley behind the beauty supply store—that was no lie.

I lied to Byron all the time. I mean daily. Hourly, by the end. When I look back, I think how crazy it all was. Lying means that you have to remember the stories you made up to cover your ass. Of course, maybe that was part of the excitement to me. Telling him I was seeing a movie with Elizabeth when I was out fucking Connor. Having to work hard to cover my tracks.

Now, Alex was asking me to lie to Jack. And from the fearful look in his eyes, I will admit that for a moment I was torn. I knew that he was right—he was a total hypocrite in even asking. I understood that. But it's all in the perspective, isn't it? Alex was horrified when I asked him to lie to Jack. It wouldn't have mattered what the subject was about. The concept of lying was the important thing to him. But his request felt different to me. He was asking me not to tell because he had no idea what the repercussions might be. Would Jack punish him, or break up with him?

This showed me how vulnerable he actually was.

When Alex shoved the prison strap in my hands, I wanted to laugh. Yeah, there were plenty of times when I had wanted to beat him, to fuck with him, to take him down not only one peg, but several. But now wasn't one of those times. How can you hurt a man who has just asked you to fall in love with him?

No, that's the wrong question. Jack would easily have been able to whip me after a similar encounter. So the difference is more fundamental than that. I'm no top.

"Please, Sam."

"I'm not going to tell him a thing," I assured Alex, after a moment. Relief flooded through him, visibly. But then I added, "You're going to come clean yourself."

His shoulders sagged. "What do you mean?"

"You tell Jack. You say what you want. What you need. Otherwise, this is all going to be too tangled to fix."

Alex shook his head. "He wants to be with you. That's clear."

"Yeah? You think so?" There was a hard edge in my voice. "He loves me," I told him. "He's said so. And yet he lets you touch me, punish me…" My voice trailed off. I wondered if the encounter after I had lied was what changed things for Alex. Had it been the time Jack brought him into our bedroom that made him want to be more than Jack's right-hand man? "What were you to him before he met me?"

Alex looked away quickly, but I caught the flush in his cheeks.

"Come on, Alex."

"He said not to talk to you about it."

"About…?"

"Our history. He said that he would tell you every-thing. When he felt the time was right."

I was in a soap opera filled with secrets. And now I was out in the woods with a man who could, if he wanted to, tell me all I needed to hear. Yet from the look on his face, I knew that he wouldn't. Loyalty was about the only thing Alex had.

Yet I thought I knew the answer from the look in his eyes.

"You're going to tell him," I said, my voice as stern as before. "You're going to tell him that you want to be more than a handler. An assistant."

"Yeah? And then he's going to fire me, and I'll have nothing."

"You can't fire someone you love." As soon as I said the words, I realized they were true. Jack loved me. I was sure of it. But he loved Alex, as well. In his own way. In his own fucked-up way, I should say.

I've talked so much about Brock. And I know that it's ancient history. Beyond ancient. Right? But that relation-ship is what everything is based on for me. Everything I know. And maybe you're supposed to have nice sweet love for your first time. Maybe you're supposed to go out with the clean-cut Christian neighbor who brings you home on time and sits at Sunday dinner next to your parents. The one who picks fresh violets for your anniversary. But I had the hoodlum instead. And I learned from my first time around that love isn't something you can capture in a Hallmark card. It's not clean. And it's not easy. If being in love with Jack meant learning to find a place for Alex, I was willing to go there.

But suddenly, I was willing to do something else, as well.

Alex was pitiful at this moment. Head in his hands. Nearly crying. He'd been with Jack for years, through various girlfriends, I could guess, and nothing like this had ever come up with him before. I stood and looked down at him. Taller for once.

"Stand up," I said, and he gazed up at me, hesitated for a moment, and then stood.

"Drop your slacks."

Now, he gave me the most incredulous look.

"You offered. I'm taking you up on it." I spoke harshly, through gritted teeth, and Alex obeyed, unbuckling his belt, lowering his slacks. He was wearing striped blue-and-white boxers, and I was the one to pull those down. I didn't bother with his new toys. I pulled the belt out of his slacks and used that, doubled up. This made it worse, somehow. I knew what I was doing. (Yes, I just told you that I wasn't a top. But like people say, there are levels of sexuality—fluctuations on the Kinsey scale. I think there are levels, ranges, of submission. If you know how to bend over, then you also know how to take control.)

I striped him, not hesitating when the lines bloomed

dark pink on his pale skin. When the angry welts formed. He took the blows like a pro, and I was sure he had at least as much experience at submitting as I did. Jack had to use someone to take out his aggression on between his chosen subs. Alex fit that part to perfection.

I don't know where the power came from. And I don't even know why it was so important that I marked Alex. I only knew that I had to do this. Had to.

I whipped him hard, the way Jack would have had he been in my place. All the frustration and the aggression I'd been feeling for weeks came out in the strokes on Alex's naked skin. And each blow turned me on more than I can say. So this was what being in charge felt like. Pretty fucking nice, I'll admit. How bizarre that Alex had brought me out there to punish me, when I was the one who ended up in position of top dog. That's L.A. for you. Things are never what they seem.

"I'm supposed to meet him at that sushi place?" I asked, dropping the belt, breathless from the exertion. Alex slowly pulled up his slacks, and I watched him wince, and that gave me nearly unbelievable pleasure. I could have come in seconds if I'd stuck one hand down my panties and stroked my clit.

"Yeah. In Santa Monica."

"Drop me back at the apartment," I told him. "You're going to meet Jack instead."

Once more, Alex's shoulders sagged.

"He doesn't want to see me. He wants to see you. Your haircut. Your outfit."

"I'll still have the haircut later on tonight. I'll wear the same clothes. None of that matters."

"He's going to be upset," he said, and I grinned, unable to help myself.

"Yeah?" I asked, taunting him. "Well, you're prepared. You've got all those brand-new devices to give him as a peace offering."

Alex looked at the bundle on the ground, and he shook his head.

"Come on," I told him. "We can't go back to everything being the way it was. You'll resent me. Hate me. If not today, then soon. And I won't be able to trust the things you say, won't know whether you're telling me something Jack wants, or something you want. You have to go meet him. And you have to tell him you want more, and that you asked me, already. And that I need to know where Jack stands."

Alex closed his eyes for a moment, as if considering. When he looked at me once more, his eyes were blazing. I saw fear, and I saw power, struggling within.

"And when he asks what my response was, you take him back to the men's room, and you show him that." I nodded to his ass and stepped forward. I then stroked his rear once, and I felt him relax, slightly. "Then tell him I'm home. Waiting..."

Chapter Twenty-Five:
Waiting

I don't know if it's true or not for most people, but I do know that pacing around the apartment had a dim effect on my psyche. Had I done the right thing sending Alex off in my place? I was taking a monumental risk. Jack had prepared this intricate sex game for me, with one carefully chosen photo leading to the next. And rather than end at the predestined conclusion—which I was guessing was kinky sex in the back alley behind the sushi restaurant—Alex and I had turned the game upside down.

Sure, I worried about Alex, too. I'm not a totally cold-hearted bitch. But I worried for myself more. I thought I knew Jack by now, understood a bit of the way he was wired. You could disagree with him, say his opinions were wrong—whatever—but you had to use a respectful tone of voice. Jack commanded respect at all times.

Had I disregarded that by willingly changing his plans?

I supposed I would find out soon.

Darkness fell, and there was no word from either man.

And then I heard Jack enter the apartment, and I hurried down the hall from where I was pretending to work. I still had on my fabulous new outfit, and I'd primped for at least an hour in the mirror, recreating the exact way Matteo had styled my hair. But Jack didn't seem to notice.

"Where the fuck were you?"

In a heartbeat, I understood. Still, I tried my best to act natural.

"Didn't Alex say?"

Jack was already in motion, my wrists in his grip, hauling me toward the bedroom. I stumbled along next to him, feeling his fury come off him in waves.

"Didn't he, Jack? Didn't he tell you?"

This was the angriest I'd ever seen Jack. He didn't speak. Simply stripped my clothes away. I stood entirely still as he pulled my shirt over my head, and he caught me off balance as he pushed me back onto the bed to undo my boots.

"He didn't show up, did he?" I asked stupidly. Why hadn't I thought of that as a possibility? I was so sure Alex would be drawn to confess, the way I am always drawn to confess, to beg forgiveness, to be absolved.

Jack remained silent, and in moments I was naked. Deep inside myself, I felt prepared to take whatever Jack had to give. But I wanted my chance to defend my actions.

"Please," I started, as he came forward with the cuffs. "Listen, Jack."

"I sat there for an hour," he said, and once more I could feel the heat of his rage. If I believed in auras, Jack's would have been blood red.

"He was supposed to meet you," I told him, speaking quickly now, not sure how long Jack would listen. "He had something to tell you."

"A message from you?"

"No, Jack. It's not about me this time. Not at all."

The cuffs were on. Jack was binding me exactly how he wanted, my arms above my head, ankles spread wide apart and fastened with thick leather straps. I could feel tears in my eyes, but not from fear. This wasn't right. It wasn't fair. I had to explain. And yet I wanted Alex so badly to be the one to tell. Now, I was doing to him what he'd done to me. I was ratting him out. But really, he'd left me no other choice.

"Why weren't you there?" Jack asked, his voice smooth now that I was bound. He seemed to have regained control of himself. And although I sensed the emotions right under the surface, I also saw that this was my opportunity to explain.

"Jack, look. Just listen for a second." He'd begun rifling through his wardrobe of toys, and I didn't want to fight for his attention with the various crops and canes, paddles and slappers, floggers and belts. When he turned to face me, for a moment, I felt relief.

"Alex told me something today. In confidence. He told me something, and I said that he needed to tell you, too. I wanted him to meet you for dinner to talk to you. I thought that was the best way to handle the situation."

"You're choreographing things now?"

"No, Jack. Wait. Listen. It was important." I wished my hands were free so I could hold them up, gesture, show him. As it was, I begged with my eyes and my words.

"What was so important that you disobeyed a direct command?" A thin black crop danced in his hands. Before I could respond, he'd slashed it through the air once, catching the fullest part of my ass. I cringed and bit down on a moan, and Jack struck again, in the same place, giving me no chance to recover. Again, the crop came down, and I fought within myself to figure out what to do next. I didn't want to sell out Alex. I wasn't feeling vindictive toward him, but I also didn't need to take on his punishment.

Jack was working faster now. Harder. And the pain flooded through me. I tried to figure out what I should be saying, doing, but the crop made thinking difficult. Jack striped me, and I took each blow. I had disobeyed, after all. Regardless of the fact that I was trying to help, trying to make the right decision, I had gone against Jack's requests. Then he dropped the crop and I saw him reach for a cane. He set the weapon down by my head, where I could look at it, while he went searching for another tool. When he came toward me again, he had a bright-red ball gag in his hands.

Oh, fuck, fuck, fuck. My desire to help Alex was fading quickly.

"He loves me." I blurted the words out without thoughts now, knowing that if I didn't make Jack understand quickly, he would render speech impossible, and it might be hours before we could talk normally once more.

"He what?" Jack didn't move, and I knew I had a little more time.

"He asked me if I thought I could love him."

"And you said..." I looked back over my shoulder. Jack's eyes were the darkest blue I'd ever seen. Nearly black, as if the pupils had swallowed up all the light.

"I didn't say *yes* and I didn't say *no*. Jack, I told him he had to talk to you. That he had to tell you."

Jack leaned against the wooden wardrobe. He seemed taken aback by my news.

"I'm sorry, Jack," I said, and now the tears that had

threatened to fall spilled free. "I'm sorry I disobeyed you. I shouldn't have changed your plans. I didn't know what to do. He said those things, and I was confused…"

Jack stayed silent, and I felt hopeless, and then, to my total shock, he smiled. It wasn't an eerie, dark grin; it was a real smile. As if something he'd been planning had come to unexpectedly early fruition.

"I don't know why he didn't meet you," I said into Jack's silence.

"Because the boy was scared." He spoke the words with some satisfaction.

"So where do you think he is?"

"If I know Alex, he's with Juliette. Taking his punishment before confessing his sins." Jack seemed to be speaking from experience. But while he seemed at ease, my head was spinning. Why was this good news to Jack? Did he want Alex to be in love with me? Nothing made any sense.

Jack came forward and petted me, stroking my new haircut, ruffling it up with his hand.

"You look good," he said.

"Yeah?" Confusion left me reeling.

"I knew that cut would suit you. I was waiting at the restaurant to see, and when you didn't show up, I thought you were pulling another one of your stunts. It never occurred to me that Alex was pulling one of his. But I should have known. He'd never have let you run off today. He was in charge of your every moment." His hand moved from the top of my head down my spine toward my ass. His touch was rough, but friendly, the way you'd stroke a big dog. "I've been working so hard," Jack continued, "that I didn't consider other options for why you weren't waiting at the restaurant, sake in place."

Now, he lifted the gag once more, and fear returned.

"You did the right thing, Sam," Jack said softly as he buckled the gag between my lips. "But that doesn't mean you won't be punished for disobedience." He lifted the cane and let the tip follow the route his fingers had taken moments before, tracing down my spine before coming to rest on my ass.

"I'll deal with Alex later—we will, together—but now, it's you and me…"

Chapter Twenty-Six:
The Chain

Jack hadn't even raised the cane once when we heard the knock. The sound wasn't loud, but loud enough. I think we both realized what the low rapping meant at the same time: Alex.

It was odd that he was knocking. I knew that right away. Alex had a key. And he'd never had any problem barging into the apartment in the past for any reason at all. Jack set down the cane, but left me bound. He didn't hurry down the hall the way I would have, curiosity driving me onward. He walked at his normal, even pace. I heard the door open, heard the low sound of male voices, and wondered like hell what was going on.

In moments, Jack was back, and this time he did set me free: the gag, the handcuffs, the ankle restraints.

"Get dressed," he said, and his tone was more tender than it had been moments before. "I need your help."

I dressed quickly, not in the fancy sex-charged clothes I'd purchased earlier in the day, but in a wrecked pair of old Levi's and one of my favorite formfitting long-sleeved shirts. This one a lipstick red. Then I hurried after Jack, still wondering what was up. Had it not been Alex at the door? Had it been someone from Jack's office? A delivery person, a messenger?

No. It was Alex. Slumped in Jack's favorite chair. Head in his hands.

You'd think that a person couldn't change his appearance that much in a few hours. But Alex had managed. He looked totally disheveled, shirt untucked, slacks rumpled. And it took me a moment to realize that he was drunk. Seriously drunk. I could hear Jack in the kitchen, and from the sounds of water running and beans being ground, I understood he was making a pot of French roast.

I sat on the edge of the low coffee table looking at Alex. So this was the result of letting loose your emotions after keeping them under wraps for so long. Alex had been the perfect tool. And, the funny thing is, I truly don't mean that as an insult. I mean it as a compliment. Jack had relied on Alex for years, had trusted him with his most treasured possessions—both monetary, like his cars and his houses, and romantic, like me. And Alex had risen to the challenge every time.

But now, he was broken.

I wondered whether I should say something. Or go forward and comfort him. In some respects, I didn't know Alex well enough to put my arms around him, to draw him close to me. How bizarre was that? Here was a man who had been extremely intimate with me in so many ways, and yet I knew almost nothing about him. Didn't know his middle name. Or where he went to high school. Or how many siblings he had. Didn't know him well enough to cuddle next to him on the big chair and surround him with my heat.

Silence screamed all around us. There was nothing for me to say.

Jack reemerged with a cup of steaming coffee, and when he looked at me, I saw that for once, he didn't seem to know what to do. We weren't acting properly the way characters should. I moved closer to Alex, so that I was right in front of him, and I pulled his hands away from his face.

"You didn't make it to dinner," I said trying my best for a light tone of voice. "So where have you been?"

He shut his eyes tight, as if trying to remember, and when he opened them again, he looked at me. I could tell that he was trying hard not to look at Jack. "I don't know," he said at first, but then he quickly named a place. A bar in Hollywood.

"You drive here?" Jack asked, his voice rough.

"No, I walked." Alex blinked hard and then looked at me. "You told him?"

And for the first time that evening, I saw a bit of myself in Alex. That time with Byron when I'd gotten drunk at his father's house, choosing to spend a night on the cold marble floor by the commode rather than face Byron's wrath. I was surprised to realize this, but Alex hadn't had the guts to have a man-to-man talk with Jack. And yet, he was here, wasn't he? He hadn't chickened out entirely.

"Yeah," I said finally. "Yeah, I told him." I wanted to explain further. I wanted to say to him, *What else could I do, you bastard? You left me no fucking choice?* But this didn't seem the time to further harass Alex. Not in his current state.

Alex swallowed, and then he looked back at the floor.

I wondered why Jack wasn't saying anything. Why he wasn't forcing his way into the conversation. I gripped Alex's hands in mine, holding them tight. "Alex, I only told him a little bit. You have to tell him the rest yourself. You have to explain."

He pulled his hands free and then reached into his pocket, drawing out a ring of keys. He set them down on the edge of the coffee table, and my heart sank. I saw what he was doing, where he was going, and I ached for him.

"I came to drop them off," he said, and when he looked back at me, I wondered if he was as drunk as I'd first thought. Was he putting on an act? His eyes looked clearer now. I reached for the coffee from Jack and handed over the mug. Alex took a sip and then held the cup between both hands.

"Don't do this," I said. "Come on, Alex. Tell him."

"Your car is fine," Alex continued. "It's in valet. They'll hold it for you."

"Alex—" Why wasn't Jack stopping him? Why was I the only one who seemed to be feeling any real sort of emotion? I wanted to cry. And then I wanted to scream. To throw things. To shake these two men up. Are all men like this? I wanted to yell at them. Unable to have an honest discussion about things that matter. Not sports or work or cars. But love and emotions and sex.

"I'll pick up my things from Malibu tomorrow," Alex continued. "I'm sure you won't have any problems finding another…"

"What?" I demanded, sick to death of this fucked-up scene. "Finding another what? You're going to say 'assistant,' but you know you're not an assistant. Not only an assistant anyway. You know that." Why the fuck was Jack just standing there, like something carved from stone?

Why was Alex reciting this idiotic resignation speech? Half-slurred, half-mumbled. It was insane. "He's not going to replace you."

"He has to."

"But why?"

"Because I can't do this anymore." Alex's voice was pleading. I heard Jack move behind me, and I was surprised to see him pouring a shot of whiskey. "I can't." Alex turned, directing his voice toward Jack. "I'm sorry, Jack—"

I realized that this didn't have anything to do with me, did it?

Jack didn't turn around. He downed the liquid in a single shot, and then poured another. And I got lost in an image from back in time.

The first threesome I had was with two guys I knew from college, Jarred and Mark. I'd hung out with Jarred all year long, playing video games in his room, watching movies on his TV. He was a junior and he had an extremely uptight sorority girlfriend, but he liked me to sleep in his bed when she wasn't around. And one night near the end of the school year, we found ourselves off campus, studying at another friend's apartment. And we started drinking. Tequila. We even went out and bought more tequila when we killed the first bottle. I remember trying uselessly to match these two boys shot for shot. I remember going to the bathroom at one point during the evening and being unable to redo the buttons on my 501s afterward. I remember being sandwiched between these handsome studs—boys who had been buddies since high school—and there was almost unbelievable pleasure at being the link between them. A necessary link. They couldn't have done the things they did if I hadn't been in the room, on the bed. In the morning, along with my first hangover, I woke up with a huge bruise on my chest. Mark had a cast on one hand, and it must have come down on me hard during the night.

After that, we weren't friends anymore. I wasn't upset at them. I didn't feel guilty. Not really. But things were different. I heard from someone else later on, that the boys were no longer friends either. Had I done that somehow?

Had I done it again, to Alex and Jack? Was this my fault?

"Jack—" Alex said. "Jack—"

And Jack turned around. "Why, Alex? You owe me that."

Alex didn't look away this time. "I don't know. It's different."

"From what?"

"From any of the other times, Jack. It's different. It's different with her."

No, I was wrong. It was about me. I wanted the whiskey.

"You love her?" Jack's voice burned as cold as his eyes.

"Damn it, Jack. Don't you fucking get it?" I looked over at Alex, surprised by his tone of voice, yet thinking that I'd guessed correctly. He was playing drunker than he actually was. "Jesus fucking Christ, Jack. I don't love her." Oh, god, and I saw it coming. Even if Jack didn't. I saw it. And I couldn't look away. I had to watch every second. Alex's voice softened, but his eyes stayed locked on Jack's. "I love you."

I got up then, and I walked to the bar, snagged a bottle, and headed down the hall.

You can't fuck with people's hearts and not expect fire-works.

You can't keep someone on a short leash and not expect to be bitten.

And I'd been right in my first guess after all. This drama wasn't about me. What had Alex been going on about at the park? Could I love him? He didn't want me to. Not really. What he wanted was a place. A place in the mix, a point in the triangle. He wanted what he'd always wanted: a share of Jack's heart.

·

Chapter Twenty-Seven:
Trust

Did everything make sense?

Yeah, finally. Or rather—well, almost.

Was the confession a relief?

Hmm. Not sure how to answer that. I'd known there was something more. Some powerful connection between the two men in my life. There couldn't not be. Not the way they acted. And yes I have an extremely active—I'd even say rampant—imagination. And yes I'd seen Jack interact physically with Alex before. But I hadn't gone to this place in my head, to this fantasy world featuring Alex in love with Jack, and all that not-so-simple four-letter word might mean.

The truth was that Jack hadn't told me any of his secrets. I assumed that he would at some point. I thought he'd sit me down and break open the vault, the way I had once long ago with Byron. And I was planning on doing my part not to let history repeat itself. No matter what Jack told me, I would be supportive. I would give him what he needed.

Yet I hadn't guessed that what he needed might not be only me. He might need Alex, too.

That night, Jack and Alex sat up in the living room talking. I could hear the lull of their voices, but I didn't eavesdrop. This was theirs. All theirs. I didn't bother trying to write—what would be the use?—and I didn't bother trying to sleep. Not for a long time. Instead, I refolded the clothes in my drawers, reorganized my lipsticks, my nail polishes. Played my all-time favorite songs to put myself at ease. Basically, I did all of the tricks I always do when my mind won't shut up.

I had come late to this game. That's what I understood the most. I'd been waiting for the secrets to spill naturally. I was trying to do things right for once.

Early on, when I'd moved in with Byron, I'd read a poem he wrote. It was in his journal, but the journal was open on his desk. It was clearly about me, my black hair, my being nineteen. And it was beautiful. I wish I could remember the words today. When I told him how much I loved it, he turned on me. Yet again, I had done something to disappoint and to displease. Every one of those types of interactions had kept me from pursuing the truth between Jack and Alex.

And now, they were out in the living room....

The liquor helped. It made me feel warm all over. I drank straight from the bottle, reveling in the sensation. I am, at my heart, vice afflicted. I enjoy liquor from a pocket flask, the thrill of getting a tattoo on a whim. I take great pleasure in not getting enough sleep, but then waking my body with too much caffeine. Ultimately, the drink made me unable to continue my puttering devices because I was causing more havoc than I was fixing. And then, when it was too late to call it late any longer, when it was early, the bedroom door opened, and Jack came in.

He looked worn. Not sad. Not demolished. Not demoralized. But worn. And he sat down on the edge of the bed and rubbed one hand over his face and down along the strong line of his jaw, and I could hear the scrape of his palm against his evening beard. He looked at me, and he seemed to easily assess my own status. I was drunk. Drunker, probably, than Alex had actually been earlier in the night.

Jack laughed. Not mean. Not caustic. Not bitter. He laughed, as if this were icing on his cake. Par for the course, given the way his evening had ended up. He came over and took me in his arms and kissed me. Hard. Just kissed me. I can hear the sound of his laughter in my head. I can feel his lips on my own. I can see the room if I close my eyes tight. I can feel the beating of his heart against mine.

There was gentleness in his eyes as he tucked me into bed. There wasn't sadness. I wasn't scared. There was only tenderness, as he bent to kiss my forehead.

Still, I tried, tried to ask what had happened. What was going on?

"Sh, baby," he said.

"I'm sorry I didn't meet you tonight," I said, focused, as ever, on what *I'd* done wrong. Should I have gone to the restaurant after all, at least showed up to make sure Alex had made it? This was an easy infraction to apologize for in hindsight. "I'm sorry I made you worry."

He shook his head. "Sleep it off. We'll talk in the morning."

In the morning, Jack played nurse to the two of us. Alex had fallen asleep on the sofa, and Jack had covered him up with the soft poppy-red blanket. He left coffee next to

Alex, but didn't wake him, and brought a cup down the hall to me, where I sat in bed wishing the room wouldn't sway quite so much.

"I have to go to work," he said, and when I looked at him, I realized his strength once more. How much sleep could he possibly have gotten? An hour? Two? And now he was off to work, where he would have to be completely focused on life outside of our twisted realm.

"Talk to Alex when he gets up. He'll fill you in. I'll try to stop by at lunch, but I don't know..."

He kissed my forehead, stroked my hair.

"Tell me it's all okay," I begged, remembering in a landslide everything that had happened the night before.

"It's all okay," he assured me. "At least, it will be." And he was out the door.

I slept most of the morning, and when I got up, Alex was out on the balcony, wearing a white T-shirt and the rumpled pants he'd had on the previous evening. This in itself was shocking. The old Alex would have pulled out the iron from the guest-room closet and done a necessary touch-up before allowing himself to be seen. The new Alex seemed perfectly satisfied to be wearing yesterday's clothes as he watched the cars rumble by on Sunset Boulevard.

I stared at him from the doorway, and then walked outside barefoot to join him.

"If your head feels anything like mine, than you have my apologies," I said.

"I'm the one who owes you an apology." Alex looked over at me and smiled. It was weird to be alone with him. The last time we were alone he'd asked if I could love him. The last time we'd been alone, I had whipped him. He seemed to be recalling the same images, because he shook his head, looking half-embarrassed, half-unsure.

"Jack said you'd tell me...."

Alex sat down at the little table, and I took over his spot, leaning against the railing.

I didn't know what Jack had actually meant. Was Alex going to tell all the secrets I'd wondered about from the start? Or was he only going to tell me what had happened the night before? I stared over at Alex, but I didn't hurry him. Clearly, he'd talk when he was ready. When he was, he said, "It wasn't supposed to happen like that."

"What wasn't?"

"My little confession."

"Confessions never happen the way you think. Or the way you'd like." That's the truth, isn't it?

"For a while, I imagined something else. Jack between women. The two of us talking. And me saying what I wanted to say." He stared at me. "Then you came along."

I swallowed hard.

"I'm not blaming you. Don't think that. I only mean, you were different. Jack's been with loads of girls over the years. But he's never moved one in before. I guess the thing is that he's never been really serious."

What was Alex saying?

"I waited, at first, to see if something else would happen. If you would flee. Not many people could take that sort of intensity, you know? From the start. He was testing you, I think. Letting you know what it means to be with him. See if you could handle the whole deal. And you kept hanging in. Holding your own. Then that night, the other night, when he let you watch...that's when I knew I had to say something."

I understood in a flash what he was talking about. Letting me see Jack whip him. "Had he done that to you before?"

Alex looked away. I was trained from years of journalism classes and working on newspapers to always keep the subject talking. But maybe it was better if I let him talk. If I didn't ask questions, he would be able to continue at his own pace. Yet when he didn't immediately keep going, I couldn't keep silent.

"What did you talk about last night?"

"I resigned, you know. I told him I couldn't work for him any longer. Not like this. Not as some third arm, to reach out and touch you when he wasn't there. To spank you, or paddle you, or fuck with you, and then leave."

For the first time, I wondered what Alex did afterward? Where did he go when he wasn't with the two of us? After he used a belt on me, did he find some other person in a pub—boy or girl—to act out the rest of his aggression on? Or did he search for some nameless Dom to take care of him? Jack had thought Alex was with Juliette. Was she his favorite surrogate? The one he submitted to, the one he craved?

"Jack's an odd duck," Alex said. "He's at a place in his life where he doesn't want any bullshit. That's why he behaved the way he did with you right away. If you were playing, he wanted to know. If you were one of these girls who needed a spanking over her fantasy Daddy's lap, he would have sent you on your way. He doesn't want a normal life. He doesn't want the American dream. He's got everything he needs professionally. He's decided to create the world he wants romantically. I think for all these years he's been looking for someone like you."

"What do you mean?"

"Not only a sub. But someone smart. Someone who has her own world, as well. You write. He likes that. You're going somewhere, which means you're not relying on him to entertain you 24/7. You're not a princess."

Maybe Jack and I had gotten to the same place at the same time. When I left Byron, I'd said good-bye to all those things I'd thought I was supposed to have. Supposed to want. The station wagon and the house in suburbia. The dinners at the in-laws'. The brunches at the country clubs.

"He was tired of the dating merry-go-round. Starting from scratch each time. So for a while, he's simply been going to Juliette. Playing there, where he knows he can find what he wants. Every once in a while, he's hooked up with a girl for a little bit longer, but none of them captivated his interest the way you did."

This was all fascinating. But I still didn't understand where Alex was going to fit in.

"I've been there the whole time. Since I was in college. I've been watching and learning. Doing everything I could to assist him any way he needed. Look, Sam, I didn't love him from the start. Don't think that. I was mesmerized by his world. It meshed with the things that I liked. But I had no idea it existed on the level that Jack takes things to. I was fine being the assistant in the past. The hired help. Because who else lives a life like this?"

I thought for a moment. From my experience in L.A., nobody really does live that American dream. Byron's father had left his mother for a lover, then left his lover for another, constantly trading up. Or down. But Jack was different. He wasn't doing things on the sly. He wasn't putting on a false front of a happy home life and then searching for his fantasies down back alleys. He wanted the back-alley life instead of the happy home life. Was that what Alex meant?

"Jack always made sure I was taken care of. If he

went to the club, he found someone for me, as well. If he had a girl home, he brought a second one. Or—every so often—a boy."

Alex looked at me, as if wondering whether he'd see judgment in my eyes. But really—I've worked in salons and beauty-supply stores since I was twelve. Half of my friends are gay men. I had no problem with Alex being gay—or bi—I wanted to know the relation to Jack.

"It was kinky and decadent, and for awhile, there were drugs, as well."

Another pause, but I just shrugged. Byron's best friend Beau had been a drug dealer for years before giving up cocaine in favor of a more stable job. I'd arrived at the very tail end of the drug years—but I'd heard the stories. Byron and his second stepmother getting high on coke at his older brother's wedding. Besides, Brock was a dealer, too. Strange that a nice girl like me would constantly find herself on the fringe of that world, but there you go. I've never done hard drugs—but I was in no position to frown at Alex's tale.

"I think he got tired of the chaos," Alex continued, "and he wanted something stable. Twisted, you know. Still dark. Still hard-core. But stable."

I nodded.

"And he found it in you, and for the first time, I was jealous. I had always been number one for Jack, even when he was with someone else. Nobody came close to having what you have with him. And it made me realize how I felt, and what I wanted...."

"But what do you want, Alex?"

"A place."

Like I'd said. A point in the triangle.

"What does that mean?"

He was the one to shrug now. "Honestly? I don't know. But Jack said he understood. Jack said we'll work it out." He beamed at me. "He said he couldn't imagine life without me...without either of us. We'll work it out. That's what Jack promised. And you know, I've been at his side all these years, I have to trust him."

Alex stared at me, obviously wanting me to comment. To respond. "Can you?" he asked me.

Yesterday's query was could I love him. What was today?

"Can I what?"

"Can you trust Jack?"

That was easy to answer. "Yes."

"And can you imagine something else. Something different. Something more?"

Could I? That was simple, as well. "Of course."

Byron had shattered my image of what happy home life was meant to be. Jack was offering new visions for me to experience. New ways for me to travel. And with all my heart I knew that I was ready for the ride.

Chapter Twenty-Eight:
You Can't Always Get What You Want

After that, we stood there together, in silence that is never really silent. Los Angeles can't shut up for a fucking minute. There were the regular sounds of the traffic and some random helicopter, and construction going on somewhere around the neighborhood. But Alex and I were quiet. For a long time.

I tried to imagine what Jack's plan might ultimately have been. Was he always looking to incorporate Alex in this way? Jack seemed far too smart to me to believe that he thought Alex was never going to crack.

And yet I believed that Jack was never going to crack. I believed in Jack's strength the way some people believe in God.

Because I'm a person who craves motion, I could only lose myself in the revelations for so long. When I needed more coffee, I headed inside. Folded the blanket that Alex had slept under. Straightened the remnants of the talk from the night before. I got showered and dressed, and picked up my notebook, planning on working from home in case Jack really did get time off for lunch.

Alex left to retrieve the car from the valet lot at the bar he'd been to the previous night. He was a lot like me in some respects. He couldn't stand to be idle, either. And he had no real vision of leaving Jack's employ. In all respects, Alex wanted more. Not less.

I was hard at work by the time Jack came home, and when he walked in, he smiled. Working is a good sign for me. I can't write if I'm upset. The same way I can't eat when I'm angry, or depressed, or nervous. Seeing my pen fly across the pages assured Jack that I truly was accepting the situation. He set down his jacket and came to my side, pulling the notebook from my hands, speed-reading what I'd spent the past hour creating.

"It's good," he said, placing the notebook on the table, rather than handing it back to me. "Fast paced. Energetic. I like that."

I thanked him but still waited for the rest. He had to know what an unusual morning I'd had with Alex. I expected him to comment on the situation in some way. Jack pulled my legs over his lap, sitting so relaxed with me on the sofa.

"I didn't plan it," he said after a few minutes. "You should know that."

"Which part?"

"Any of it. I didn't plan that you would be the way you are. That I would need you here with me. That knowing you were here would make the rest of my life fall into place. I didn't plan that you being here would drive Alex over the edge. And generally," he continued, "I plan everything."

I knew this to be true. From the careful black-and-white décor in his homes to the military precision of his closet, Jack kept his whole world in line.

"At first," Jack said, "I was waiting. I hoped things would go smoothly, but I had no idea. You definitely were rebounding. That was easy to see. And I didn't want to scare you off or anything, but I didn't hold back."

Exactly what Alex had said. It had all been some kind of twisted test from the start.

"And when you rose to each challenge, I became more intrigued. More sure of my decision. I didn't stop for a moment to think about how Alex was feeling. He's always been behind what I do. But he has a different emotional makeup than I do."

Was that Jack's way of saying Alex was weaker, or that Alex was more human? Alex had feelings? Where Jack was generally colder. Less swayed by emotions than by facts.

"But what does it all mean?" I asked. "Where... I mean, how...?" I didn't really know what I meant. Was Alex going to move in with us? Was he Jack's other love?

"I think acknowledging the situation was what Alex wanted. The start, anyway. He knows there are ways that I feel about you, that I'll never feel for him. I think he knows that, anyway. He's not going to sleep in our bed, if that's what you're wondering about. You won't be the filling in some sex sandwich. At least, not every day...."

I liked the image that immediately rose to the front of my mind.

"It's not something you can fix in a day. You understand that, right? We're talking long haul. So the real question is, are you willing?"

"Willing..."

"To try. To do something different. To be someone different."

"Different from what?"

"From anyone else. From all the other cookie-cutter people that you meet. From the girl who told you on your first day at college that you weren't going to have any friends if you didn't join a sorority. From your boss at the salon who said if you didn't become a born-again, you wouldn't get into heaven. Are you ready to close the door on all those other people's beliefs and rules and live the way you want to?"

Jack had an excellent memory. Both of those stories were true. So in a way, I already was doing what he was asking. By being a pornographer, I already was breaking most people's rules of conduct. But Jack wasn't talking occupation. He was talking lifestyle.

"Could you go out to dinner with both of us, feel Alex's hand on your leg under the table, feel mine caressing your face where everyone could see? Could you leave arm in arm with both of us and know that people thought you were..."

"A slut?" I interrupted, playing.

"An anything. *Anything* that they thought. What I'm really asking is whether you can forget about what other people will say, what other people want from you, and focus only on what I want?"

"Yes, Jack."

"Even if what I want is to let Alex in. I don't know how far. I don't know how much. But in. Can you do that?"

"Yes, Jack."

I am, as I've said, at my heart monogamous. And I am loyal. But Jack wanted more.

And I wanted Jack.

Yet it goes deeper than that. I grew up in a bohemian household, and all I ever wanted was normal. I wanted my dad to go to work with a briefcase, like my friends' fathers. I wanted to attend the pretty white church down the block. And I learned fairly early on that you can't always get what you want.

But maybe my 1970s schooling ran deeper than I'd thought. Maybe the hippy talk of being different, of breaking other people's expectations, of living outside the box finally sank in.

"You won't feel dirty?" Jack asked.

And I understood. Jack wasn't only asking if I was willing to obey his requests. He was asking if I could change my whole definition of what was normal. If I could look at what we did together as acceptable, as healthy, as clean and good and wholesome.

"Of course, I'll feel dirty," I told him, and he started to frown, until I said, "I always feel dirty, Jack. That's part of what I am. I felt dirty when I was with Byron because I wanted what he couldn't give me. I couldn't be the girl he hoped for. But I felt dirty even when I was with Brock, because he could give me what I wanted. Because of the very things I wanted." Those feelings weren't going to evaporate because Jack asked them to. "I don't care," I told him, feeling so lighthearted I wanted to laugh. "I don't care about other people at all. I just want you."

Jack wrapped his hand up in my hair and pulled me tight to him. He kissed me as hard as he had the night before, but this time, the kiss was leading forward. This time the kiss was the prelude. There were no answers yet. No real ones. I didn't have a clue where Alex would belong. But I was ready to find out. As I was ready to slide my body against Jack's, to feel how deliciously hard he was beneath his clothes, to rock on him, trying to make him lose control for once. Trying, in my own pale way, to take charge.

He leaned back for a moment, staring at me, understanding my mission and clearly getting a kick out of my attempt. His blue eyes were brighter as he watched me, as he let me work my body on his. I was his private lap dancer, grinding my hips forward, connecting in the fiercest way. I wanted to make him let loose. I wanted to make him come, the way I'd gotten Connor off at work. Make him come in his pants. I don't know why I thought I could. I don't even know why I tried.

Jack laughed, a dark rippling sound. Then he gripped my arms and pulled me off him, stood up and threw me over his shoulder, taking me down the hall to the bedroom...taking me to what suddenly felt like home.

Chapter Twenty-Nine:
Dr. Jack

Sure, there were times when we simply fucked. You have to understand that, right? Every so often, Jack bent me over the bed and took me from behind. Or he caught me coming out of—or going into—the shower and we reveled in watery bliss. We did it in the kitchen and on the balcony, in his car and in the garage. We were "normal" in that aspect. I mean, in the aspect that every interaction didn't involve whips and chains and potential infractions of Jack's various rules.

But I have to say that I don't get off on sweet sex. In my heart, I believe that being into BDSM has a lot in common with being gay or lesbian. I mean, I get that people might wonder how we could keep up the intensity, that shimmer of pain each and every time we did it—but that's like asking a gay man, "Don't you ever want to just fuck a woman for once?" I'm hardwired to want some sort of kink in the bedroom. It's what's in me. I don't need to cry every time I have sex. I don't need to be reduced to that liquid form of iridescent shame. But I need something more, something else besides your standard hot romp beneath the sheets.

That's the truth.

During the few times it was good with Byron, my mind took me to a different place. I told the story I needed to hear in order to gain the pleasure I craved.

So even when Jack hadn't bound me down, or pulled out a gag, or slid off his belt to make me kiss the buckle— there was still the power in him. His hand still gripped tight in my hair to pull back my head as he worked me. Or his words still teased me, taunted me, as he explained what would happen if I didn't perform exactly right. He never expected me to be something I wasn't. He never wanted me to turn into someone else.

But all of that doesn't mean Jack was never light-hearted. On this day, he carried me back to the bedroom caveman style and slung me onto the bed. I looked at him, watchful, as he headed to our closet.

Was he after one of the little costumes he'd bought me?

Or one of my sets of high-heeled slippers, with the feathers on the toe?

Did he want me to dress up like Bettie Page?

Or maybe put on the rubber catsuit, that was hell to get into and out of, but lots of fun while it was on....?

No, Jack was on a mission. He pushed to the back of the closet, reemerging with the doctor bag, and my legs clenched together in instant anticipation. Jack looked gleeful as he set the bag on the bed and started rummaging within. He hadn't actually played doctor with me. He'd let Alex have the fun. And the mood had been so skewered that night. But this was different. Jack's blue eyes shined almost mischievously as he set out the gleaming instruments.

He didn't seem to be interested in some full-on fantasy today. He didn't need me in a tie-robe. Didn't leave the room so that I could strip in privacy. He simply wanted to try out the tools, nodding for me to take off my clothes while he continued to arrange the instruments.

I watched, eyes wide, as he slid on a pair of those ultra-thin rubber gloves. They seemed to transform him, and even though he was playing lightly with me—no warnings, no cold instructions—his very posture was different.

There were hardly any words as he tried out the various devices, using cool lube to prep me before sliding a stainless-steel speculum between my nether lips, spreading me open. An instant blush turned my cheeks dark berry. Jack was inspecting me, and he took his time, his fingertips brushing my clit as if by accident. I was obviously wet, had been since he pulled out the bag—had been, honestly, since he threw me over his shoulder—but Jack didn't chide me about my arousal. He made little comments under his breath, to himself, as he "worked." And then he told me to flip over.

Being on my stomach was both better and worse. I could face away from Jack, so he wouldn't see the expressions flitting across my face. But I knew—or could guess—what was coming next, and that made me want to grit my teeth, to freeze entirely.

Once more, I felt the lube on Jack's gloved fingertips, although he probed me here slightly longer than was medically necessary, his fingertips slipping inside of me, first one, then two. I groaned and arched my hips, automatically. The next toy felt like a butt plug—Jack slid the device inside of me, and then he pulled some part of it out.

It was like a funnel—spreading my cheeks only slightly—and Jack lost interest in moments. Pulling the whole thing out and trying something new.

My heart was racing by now, and I wondered how long Jack would wait before fucking me. He had to be hard. He had to be ready. I was stripped naked and letting him probe and position me exactly how he craved.

But Jack's got an iron will. He tried out toy after toy, employing the thermometer, so that I felt as if my cheeks were now on fire. Humbled, so turned on by the way he was touching me, and so embarrassed that I was turned on. It never changes for me. I will never get over these types of reactions.

Finally, Jack seemed finished, moving aside the instruments and telling me to roll over.

I faced him, and he grinned at me, his gorgeous smile lighting his face, and then said, "Hands over your head."

Now he was binding me. But I thought he would simply fuck me. He seemed done with the toys, and there hadn't been that many others, had there? But once Jack had me in place, he pulled out a final device, a tiny spiked wheel that made me catch my breath. It looked like a miniature version of the spur cowboys wear on their boots.

"What's that for?" My voice was a whisper.

"It's a nerve stimulator," Jack said authoritatively, but I don't think any doctor has employed it precisely how Jack did, running the tiny spiked wheel over my erect nipples, so that I thrashed as much as the bindings would allow, then tracing the wheel down my belly, closer and closer to the place between my thighs.

"Jack—"

His eyebrows raised. Was I going to say "No"?

He'd taken off his gloves, and his bare fingers spread

my pussy lips and I held my breath as ever so lightly he grazed my clit with the instrument. And—fuck—I saw stars. Jack seemed to be gauging my reaction, moving the device down the insides of my thighs before tracing it back up to my pussy. The sensation was unreal. At the level he was touching me, I'd never come, but I couldn't manage to ask him for more. Those tiny little spikes were maddening. And then Jack—knowing precisely what was going on in my mind—turned the wheel on its side and dragged it across my clit like that, to give me greater contact, sending me instantly swirling into climax.

He dropped the toy immediately and climbed onto the bed, freeing his cock and fucking me in his clothes while I was still coming, pushing the limits of my pleasure beyond one simple orgasm. His cock thrust so deep into me, over and over, and I stared up at him while he fucked me, watching his face, watching the change come over him.

When he came, I came once more, from the combination of the pressure he gave me, sealing his body so tightly to mine, and from the look in his eyes as they held mine. Never leaving me. Focused on me even when the pleasure left him shaking. He demanded the same from me, the same intensity. Not allowing me to go within myself when I came. To hide. To disappear. He held me with his look alone, no words, no threats, so that we were bound together.

Bound as one.

Chapter Thirty:
Free-Falling

I had already been signed for a third novel while still finishing my second. The contract was for a detective novel, which I hoped to write in my best Raymond Chandler style. I'm a noir fan to my core.

I began my mystery without any idea of "whodunit" or what they'd done, but wanting to capture the feel of Chandler and Hammett and Delacorta, and some Elmore Leonard. I've grown as a writer over the years, in that I outline a bit better now and often have at least a general idea which of my characters will end up together. But at the start I was much more of a free-falling writer, spiraling after my characters wherever they might take me.

And Jack, Alex, and I were free-falling as well.

Not in a bad sense. Not in a dangerous, no-parachute sort of way, but in a no-stated-rules manner. I understood Alex was going to be more involved from here on. Yet there had been no town council meeting, no updated regulations posted on the wall to observe: Lifeguard Most

DEFINITELY NOT ON DUTY. The only real difference that I could discern was a more gentle quality between Jack and Alex. When Jack spoke to Alex, he seemed to be less rigid. Less the employer, more the friend.

Of course, that didn't mean he was less strict with me.

I had the freedom to write, as always, and I could travel the city without Alex hounding me. But when Jack was home, when he was in the mood, I was all his.

During this time, Jack was working hard. The way Jack worked was new to me, so many hours, so much intensity. I was used to Byron, I was used to Byron, beyond laid-back, missing deadlines. Jack was surrounded by people who worked exactly the same way he did. It didn't seem strange to them.

On what downtime he had, Jack worked me with the same intensity he brought to his career. He was focused. He never missed a beat. There are some people for whom failure is truly a four-letter word. That's how it was for Jack.

I'm devoted in my work, too. Sometimes I truly feel as if I could write and write and never stop... This is probably why I was never all that stressed about signing on for novels back to back. I wrote for hours on my mystery, taking breaks only for inspiration, driving to my favorite spots in L.A. to find areas I wanted to write about.

If you look hard enough, I've always felt, you can actually see the noir L.A. under the surface. There are plenty of places that still seem straight out of the '30s, '40s, and '50s. If you squint, you can almost see the characters from *Sunset Boulevard,* or *The Big Sleep.* Yes, much of old L.A. has been torn down, but plenty of the old-time era remains.

I'd drive to coffee shops and sit in the windows, people

watching. I'd go up to the Observatory and stand at the railing looking out at the city. Then I'd return to my work and write until my fingers ached. My breaks during this book were for food, drink, and Jack.

Not that Jack had to compete with my work. I was always ready to set down my pen when he came home. Ready to pour him a drink, or put on an outfit, or come toward him with a paddle, begging, head down, when he'd gone too long without using it on me. And too long? What is that precisely on an actual clock?

A day?

An hour?

I don't know. Can't explain the drive, the need, that overtakes me every so often. The urge that might make me dress up before Jack arrived, sliding into something long and tight and slinky or short and hot and naughty. Waiting, helpless, for Jack to walk through the door. For him to take one look at me and understand.

That doesn't mean Jack gave me what I wanted right away. It only means that he knew what I was asking for, what I craved. And knowing always gave him power— even more than he already had. He could stretch out an evening, sure that I would be the most obedient pet ever as long as he held out my fantasy in front of me. Promising me that if I behaved—if I could only behave—he would take me where I needed to go.

And then there were the times when he told me what he wanted, what his fantasy was for the evening, and I rebelled. Understanding that by not doing what he desired, I would ultimately get what I wanted.

Does that make sense?

And then there was the almost unreal time when my publisher in New York called Jack and told him to spank me, reaching through the phone lines from Manhattan to playfully explain my necessary punishment to Jack. This was the first time my work and sex life had truly collided since Nathan. I'd made a huge error: I had turned in the manuscript, but one of the two files was corrupted, and I realized that I didn't have a backup.

I had the printout. I had a previous version. But I'd made changes at the end and somehow hadn't saved them onto my computer.

This meant that I had to retype nearly one hundred pages in an extremely short time period. I'm a fast typist. Superfast. But it was a lot of work. Needless work. Stupid work. I hadn't told Jack right away, because I was mortified by the blunder. My publisher, thinking the whole thing was humorous, ratted me out to Jack, with the careful instructions that Jack was to bend me over his lap and spank the daylights out of me.

He was laughing as he said it, but Jack took the instruction to heart, catching me off guard with a little unexpected question.

"You always back up your work?"

I looked into his eyes and knew that he knew. Although I didn't know how.

"I do now," I said, trying to be lighthearted.

Jack nodded. "Let me help you remember to do so in the future."

It was a crazy kind of spanking, because I protested. Jack had said from the start that my writing was my own. That must have meant that my writing career was also my own, I thought, and therefore if I fucked up, it had nothing to do with Jack. But Jack had enjoyed his banter with my publisher, enjoyed the teasing instruction, and was determined to carry it out.

I fought at first, telling him I'd already typed up the replacement pages, had the disk ready to go out FedEx the next day.

"But why didn't you tell me about it? I could have gotten someone to type it for you."

"I didn't want—"

"To what?"

"To look like an idiot."

Jack grinned. "And how do you look now?"

My shoulders sagged. "But Jack," I tried anyway. "It doesn't have anything to do with you. With us…"

"It has everything to do with me. Everything you do has something to do with me." He'd lost his smile. "Do you understand that?"

I nodded.

"Bend over my lap."

It was the hardest hand-only over-the-knee spanking he'd ever given me, making me burn and beg. Somehow, my attitude made it worse. If I'd resigned myself from the start, I would have absorbed the pain better. But because I was angry at my publisher, angry at Jack, I ended up feeling every single blow—to both my ass and my ego.

For Jack, this was theater. Pure entertainment. For me, it was like having my mistakes put up on a billboard for all to see.

When he was done—at least, when I thought he was done—he pushed me off his lap and looked down at me. "That was for failing to back up," he said, his voice stern. "Now, meet me in the bedroom for the next round."

My eyes were wide.

"If you have to ask me why, then we're at a far different place than I'd thought."

I didn't have to ask. I knew why. I'd struggled. I'd

fought him. I hiked my jeans back up and walked toward the bedroom, growing wetter with every step I took.

Chapter Thirty-One:
Alex's Transformation

Alex was in and out of the apartment as always, working early and staying late, because Jack was the busiest he had been since we'd met. It's not that there was no physical interaction at this time. It's only that I can't really imagine writing down every time we had sex, every different way that we fucked. I've already explained my philosophy about sex—how you can have non-monotonous monogamous encounters if you keep your mind open. If you're willing to take things to a higher level.

Well, after Jack had finished the big case he was working on, he was willing.

And the next level involved Alex. Involved Alex in a brand-new role. One Friday morning, Jack took me to breakfast and described what he had in mind. He said that he felt he'd been too distracted lately with all the chaos at his job, and he wanted to spend the weekend in total relaxation. For some, this might mean a trip to Palm Springs or even a few nights at a spa.

For Jack, this meant that he wanted to "break Alex in" to a new way of thinking.

I had no idea what he was talking about. Jack explained in his own way. "Alex wants more. He's been clear about that." He stared at me for a moment, as if thinking over his past history with Alex, a history I only had the bare-bones knowledge of. "And I should have expected this type of...not rebellion, but request for extension for some time. I know you don't have a problem bringing him into our relationship. He's already there. Right?"

I nodded. Yeah, Alex was there. He was there to make sure that I followed Jack's rules. He was there to use Jack's belt on me if he felt I was out of line. He was there, as he'd always been, a baby Dom.

"But the thing is, Alex doesn't really know what he wants. He switches in a way that I've never fully under-stood. I guess it's why he's always been so appealing to me. He likes to play with both men and women—although he does have specific types and tastes. He likes to be both a Dom and a sub. He's malleable. But this weekend, I want to cast him in one specific role. I want this to be Alex's time to fully experience a sub nature. And I want you to help me tame him."

His eyebrows went up as he looked at me, as if asking silently if I were game.

Of course, I was game. Think of what I had before Jack. Total lack of physical and emotional input from my ex. Byron punished me by not speaking to me. By not touching me. He made me feel as if I truly were one of the least attractive creatures on the planet. I'm smart enough to know that it wasn't true—because Byron held himself in such high esteem, why would he want to stay with a troll? But I was so beaten down by the time I left that it really took ages for me to be able to look in the mirror and not see myself through his critiques.

Now, here was Jack, asking me to partner with him. Offering a range of yet unknown pleasures. "Yes, Jack," I said automatically. "Whatever you want...."

As he began to describe his plan, I felt my heart start to race. I'd read enough Victorian erotica to know where he was going when he described the outfit he wanted me to buy for Alex. And I'll admit that this type of fetish had never been forefront in my own personal fantasies. But the idea of teasing Alex, of—as Jack had said—taming him, made my panties wet.

Jack had a list:

high-heeled shoes in Alex's size
ruffled panties
a pretty pinafore
a harness that would fit my slim waist.

I had the makeup, of course, and the minor skills to use it.

"Where's Alex now?" I asked.

"He's doing errands in Malibu today," Jack explained. "He knows to come by tonight. He doesn't know he'll be staying the weekend."

I looked back at the list, thinking of how I'd feel as I visited the different fetish stores, as I purchased the items Jack requested. Jack paid the breakfast bill and drove me back home. He had to hurry to get to work, but he hesitated a moment with the engine running. "You're ready for this?" Jack asked, looking closely at me.

I glanced at the list—the word *harness* standing out boldly to me—and looked back at Jack, responding like a soldier in his private army. "Yes, Sir."

"I'll do my best to be home early. You have everything set for me."

"Yes, Jack," I said, wishing there was time for him to take care of me now. Wishing he could spare the few minutes for a quick fuck that would at least buy me a little breathing room. How was I going to wait all day?

"Good girl," Jack said, smiling at me, clearly guessing how aroused the whole scenario was making me. "See you tonight..."

Chapter Thirty-Two:
Shopping Spree

I was becoming a regular customer at several of the local sex toy stores. In fact, I'd almost lost my nervousness completely about walking down the fetish-filled aisles. (All right, I still blushed, but I could handle the situation.) This time, I was on a mission. I was actually being allowed the chance to see life from Alex's perspective. Jack had given me a job, and there was no way I planned on failing.

The list was bold in my mind. Everything had to fit Alex except for the harness. That was for me. And that was the only real reason I felt insecure as I wandered through the different rows. A harness was all Jack had said. But I knew what buying one would mean. I would be wearing the thing by the end of the night, and I would be topping Alex.

Swallow hard with me, if you want to feel that lump of fear in my throat. This was far out of my realm of fantasy. Pushing my personal boundaries to the extreme. What would it be like to fuck Alex? What would it be like to stand behind him, to grip his hips, to pull him back on—

On what?

Jack must have wanted me to choose a cock to go with the harness, right? He hadn't said, and I guessed that several of our toys at home would probably work. But why not be sure?

I picked the harness first, a sleek black leather one with silver buckles. The pierced, pink-haired woman behind the counter hurried over to my side to explain the benefits of the one I'd chosen. "It doesn't cover your coochie," she pointed out. "The straps go around the upper thighs, leaving your ass and your pussy exposed."

"Wow," I nodded, impressed with how much information she happily offered, and thinking back to high school, when a group of my friends and I had been assigned to do an oral report on PMS for science class, and one of us had to use the words "breast tenderness." For hours, we all stood in front of the mirror, practicing, trying to decide who could say the phrase without turning beet red. I compared that experience with this girl who had no problem at all talking to me about my coochie.

"And you'll want to choose one of these," she said forcefully, leading me to the display of dildos and gesturing at the ones she liked the best for a variety of reasons. Some were stiffer. Some vibrated. One was a pure midnight blue. One was angled to reach the G-spot. (Not a bonus where fucking Alex was concerned.) I waited for her to leave so that I could make my choice alone, but she seemed glued to me. The store was empty at this early hour, so perhaps she was bored.

Now, if I were writing a story for one of my anthologies, I would describe the sex scene the girl and I enacted in the dressing room. You can see it, can't you? This pink-haired minx would have grabbed her favorite dildo—electric violet—explained that I really couldn't make a confident choice without trying one out, and then led me to the dressing room on the lower floor. And depending on my mood, I would have written how I had fucked her up against the mirror until she screamed with pleasure. Or I would have described how she had undressed me piece by piece, bent me over the lilac marabou-trimmed chaise, and taken my "coochie."

But those are fantasy stories, and all that actually happened was that the pretty punk girl wrapped up my selections in tissue paper and handed me my silver Mylar bag and a copy of the store's catalog. "In case you want to order anything from the privacy of your home," she said, with a wink.

At the next store, I bought Alex's outfit, using my own discretion in regard to color and the amount of ruffles, keeping in mind Alex's coloring, his build, his attitude. Trying to imagine him in the clothes. I didn't want him to look ridiculous. I wanted him to look sexy.

Years ago, when I was still in school, I managed a tiny clothes store in town. One of our regular customers was a transvestite who would come in dressed entirely as a man—and looking rather hunky, actually, in a Clooney-esque sort of way—and then would change into outfits in the little dressing room, adding the shoes he'd brought with him in his briefcase. It was a bit amazing that he actually fit into the clothes. Yes, he chose the largest sizes, but how many men can buy off the rack from a ladies' store?

He only occasionally made purchases. I think the thrill was more in choosing the clothes and trying them on in a public environment. For the first few times, he simply walked around the store. Then he lied and said he was looking for something for his wife. The next time, he added that she and he were about the same size, so maybe he should try on the dress to see if it would fit her. And finally, he came out of the dressing room one day wearing one of the pretty frocks, complete with nylons and high heels.

Aside from helping buddies with their makeup before catching midnight viewings of *Rocky Horror*, this was about the sum of my experience in the dressing up men department. But I imagine it's probably a bit more than most twenty-three-year-olds have.

For Alex, I did my very best, choosing two different pairs of shoes—one stripper high, the other slightly more subdued, but still towering. Jack hadn't said anything about a wig, but I bought one—a pink one, thinking about the pretty vixen in store number one. Sometimes being fully in disguise helps. I know that.

Then I went home and started to prepare.

Chapter Thirty-Three:
To Be a Lover

Home again with my purchases and my plans, I set about turning our place into the perfect party atmosphere. I'd gone beyond the list of Jack's requirements, stopping at a stationery store to buy additional supplies. Streamers. Ribbons. I even bought silver heart-shaped balloons. We were not near Valentine's Day, but the living room and bedroom were adorned in that spirit by the time I was done.

When I was finished, I set out the dress, shoes, wig, and stockings I'd bought for Alex. And then I went to transform myself. I wanted to wear the harness under my clothes, and I'd known that meant that most of my form-fitting jeans were out. So I'd also gone to a thrift store on Melrose and bought pants that fit over the leather harness. (Shades of working in that clothes store back in school, with me in the role of the transvestite now.) I'd bought a vintage sailor top, as well, and even though Jack had not asked me to dress up for the evening, I...well, I had plans of my own.

With hours to play before Jack and Alex arrived, I took my time, fitting on the harness, cuffing the pants, choosing the perfect motorcycle boots. My hair was short now, and easy to slick back. I used black kohl pencil on my eyes, going for that rock-star androgynous look and succeeding to some degree. I didn't bind my breasts, but I put on two tight-fitting sports bras for a flattening effect. When I was finished, I had to admit, I looked good. I'm too small to be any sort of threatening male presence. Too fine-boned to pass for a real man at all. But I didn't look like me, and that was the goal.

With a bit of Jack's aftershave, I completed the job. And then I poured myself a glass of wine and waited. The rest was up to Jack. I didn't know what he would have told Alex. I didn't know how the boy was—or was not—prepared for the events of the evening. But I did know that I was growing wetter by the second.

Jack arrived home early, took one look at me, and started to laugh.

"Should I change?" was my instant response.

"No, baby, you look amazing."

"I wasn't sure—"

He pulled me to standing and spun me around. He touched my heavy belt, stroked my flat chest, nodded his admiration. "It's wonderful." He stepped back to take in the whole effect. When he kissed me, and got a whiff of his own scent, he laughed again. Clearly delighted with my transformation.

"That's what happens when you date a writer," he said as he poured himself a drink. "You give the bare outline, and a whole story emerges."

I sat back down on the sofa, pleased with the compliment, as we waited for our guest of honor to arrive.

Chapter Thirty-Four:
Like a Girl

Did I think Jack would actually let me change his plans like that? I mean, I didn't know what his plans actually were, but he'd given me a very specific list, and although I had bought every item he'd requested, I'd also bought several extraneous ones.

As I sat at Jack's side, I was aware of him staring at me. Sipping from his drink and staring. No, I'm not the first girl to try out a look like this. I'll admit, the scene in *9½ Weeks* was in my mind as I transformed myself. But was it in Jack's?

He looked without speaking for several moments, and then he said, "We've got some time."

"What do you mean?"

"Alex had a few errands of his own today. He won't be here for a bit."

I waited, knowing there was more to come.

"Walk for me."

Without a word, I stood and crossed the room,

knowing somehow what Jack wanted. To see if I had any sort of swagger. To see if I could pull off the insolence of a tough young male. Jack laughed at my stride, and I felt my face flush. But at least he found humor in my attempt at masculinity. He wasn't visibly angry or offended.

"Now, show me what you've got."

I hesitated this time, unsure.

"Show me, Samantha. Drop your trousers and show me."

I unbuckled my belt, realizing my fingernails were still painted my favorite hue—that dark blood-red Vamp. But this was the era when boys were playing with nail polish. That didn't matter so much. I worked the belt, pulled the buttons on my fly, and then lowered my jeans.

The cock, which had been molded up against my flat belly, now sprang forward.

Jack laughed harder than ever.

I hadn't wanted something realistic. The veiny ones with real-looking accessories had given me the creeps. This was beautiful. Midnight blue with swirls of white. Big, but not too big. I slid my hand along the shaft and Jack stopped laughing.

"You touch yourself like a girl." There was both disgust and pity in his tone.

"I am a girl."

"Not in that outfit. You're trying for Sailor Joe, right? Yet you grip your joint in that wimpy manner. *Oooh, look at me! I have a cock.* Christ, it's not even a cock. It's some girly toy." He'd nailed me. He was right. I had gone half the distance in my efforts, hadn't been willing to go the full route.

"Try again." His voice was cold. The rules of the game had changed.

I thought of what Jack looked like when he came on me, every so often, standing next to the bed, working his hand on his cock. The image made me seriously wet. When Jack gave himself pleasure, let himself go, finally reached his limits. And Jack had such serious self-control that I found that situation mesmerizing. Jack's hand, jerking faster and faster, touching himself harder and with more power than I'd ever dare.

With difficulty, I tried to channel that image, tried to make the vision my own. I closed my eyes and let my head go back. I stood up tall, feeling a little more powerful in my Docs than I would have barefoot, although the fact that my jeans were pooled around my ankles did limit my mobility. Concentrating, I slid my hand along the smooth plastic cock. Up and down, squeezing hard, speeding up.

"Spit on your palm," Jack whispered.

I did. Or I tried. Waiting for the inevitable, "You spit like a girl" comment to come. I could have licked my palm. I could have unbuckled the toy and deep-throated it with finesse. But this was different. This was all at once a lesson—work rather than play.

"Jesus," Jack said, and I opened my eyes, watching as he stood up from the sofa and came to my side. He pushed me back against the wall, spit into his own palm and started to work my cock for me. And in instant, I felt as if it really were my cock. As if I were connected to this toy, or really, as if I were part of an X-rated version of *The Velveteen Rabbit* and the synthetic cock had somehow turned real.

Jack's eyes burned into mine as he stroked me, forcing the connection between the two of us. I could imagine us somewhere else. In the back room of a club, Jack manhandling me. Others watching. An audience forming because of our heat. Or out behind some bar, in the parking lot, Jack using his own spit to lube me up, knowing that in seconds he was going to have to stand aside, to watch me come on the dirt.

And then another image, one that made my heart seem to still. Jack doing this. Exactly this. To Alex. And right then, as I stared at Jack, wondering if he could see the questions swirling in my eyes, the door opened and in walked Alex.

My breath caught. Each time Jack's hand pumped my cock, he pressed the base of the toy back against my clit. And each time I felt that connection I thought I would come. He didn't stop. He didn't turn or say a word. He kept going, pausing only to add a bit more spit to his palm, so that I felt he was greasing me.

Alex froze. I'm sure some wiseass comment was on the tip of his tongue, but maybe he caught a look at Jack's face, and that stopped him. He was able to shut the door behind him, and then he stood totally still, and I knew he was waiting for instructions.

"You're going to come, boy?" Jack crooned to me, but teasing somehow. Taunting me for doing this in the first place. For adding my own bits of fantasy to a script he'd fully realized already in his head.

"Yeah, Jack."

"Then come."

My knees would have buckled if Jack hadn't used one hand to pin my shoulder against the wall, holding me in place. The climax was almost frighteningly intense. Embarrassingly so, as I was being watched closely by the two men in my life. And then it was over, and Jack let me go, and I hiked up my jeans and sank down to the floor, letting the wall support me now.

"You even come like a girl," Jack said, as he poured himself a fresh drink.

I didn't answer that. I didn't have anything to say.

Chapter Thirty-Five:
Blurring the Lines

See? You can be dead sure that you are into one thing, focused on that concept solely, and then be demolished when something else turns you on. In all the years I dated Byron, I never thought of dressing in drag, of buying a harness, of stroking my synthetic cock in front of him. Never even remotely imagined demanding that he deep-throat my new toy, or suggesting that I get out a bottle of lube and have a serious romp between his pillowy cheeks.

I think he would have passed out at the idea. Or maybe had a heart attack on the spot and died.

But with Jack, all things were possible.

Like the fact that he didn't have to say a word to Alex, that Alex came forward, grabbed me up in his arms, whispered to me that I was so fucking sexy. "Didn't think you could look like that," he said, eyes roaming over my outfit. "You're such a girly-girl usually."

And he was right. I am. But on this night, I was some-thing else. How odd that I'd thought of the encounter as

"Alex's Transformation," when it wound up being mine, as well. Jack motioned to Alex, and he nodded, grabbing my hand, pulling me back to the bedroom. Jack didn't follow, and I realized that I was the one who was going to have to explain the next part of the scenario to Jack's right-hand man. At least I thought I was. But as soon as Alex saw the purchases spread out on the bed, he seemed to understand.

"You know where he sent me today?" Alex asked.

I shook my head.

"A salon. For a wax job."

I watched as Alex peeled off his clothes, revealing the smooth expanse of his broad chest. He had also very recently shaved, not relying on the early morning's visit with the razor. I sat on the edge of the bed, surprised at how quickly, how willingly, he got naked. Had Jack prepped him? Or was Alex such an obedient assistant that he would do whatever Jack requested of him? Even when that request wasn't verbally given?

"What's next?" he said, staring now at me.

I handed over the panties, and his cheeks turned ever so slightly pink as he pulled them on. "You had to get ruffles," he said softly.

"They were specially requested," I told him.

Alex nodded, waiting for me to pass over the white pinafore, like something from *Alice in Wonderland*. Or something from an acid dream. A pinafore with ruffles, as well, but one in a size that would fit the well-built man standing feet from me. He pulled the dress over his head, and then gave me a mock curtsy, and I started to giggle.

"You think I'm pretty?"

"No. Not really."

He looked hurt. "Well, why the fuck not?"

199

"You're not done." I handed him the wig, and he took it and stood in front of the dresser, adjusting the wig over his short blond hair. He was looking more like a large doll at this point than a man in girl's clothing, or an actual girl. But I hadn't gotten the feeling that Jack wanted Alex to look like a girl. He seemed to be making a point. Showing Alex what he could make him do. And Alex was willingly playing along. It would take far greater skill than what I possessed to make Alex look passably female.

When he had the wig in place, I came to his side and did the makeup, going for a lighter version of Tim Curry's look in *The Rocky Horror Picture Show.* No whiteface, but plenty of eye shadow, lipstick, rouge. Then I took a step back and admired the outfit.

"Oh, wait," I told him. "Shoes!"

I'd gotten the two pairs, but now I realized that I'd forgotten nylons. Quickly, I rummaged around through my drawer. He'd never fit into my panty hose, but he easily slid on a pair of stockings, ones that had a self-sticking band at the top—rendering garters unnecessary. Once he'd slid the stockings over his silky smooth legs—he'd had the full wax job here, as well, I noted—I offered him the choice of heels. To my surprise, he chose the super-high ones, and he walked gracefully in them, making me wonder if perhaps this wasn't Alex's first time in drag.

"Now what?" he asked, gazing at his own reflection.

"I guess I bring you back down the hall to Jack."

"He didn't say what he was going to do?"

I shook my head.

"Did he dress you himself?"

I shook my head again. "I was inspired," I told him, "by what I'd bought for you."

But before we could return to Jack, the bedroom door

opened and my man—*our* man—entered the room. He took a moment to drink in the new Alex, before sitting on the chair in the corner. He still had a whiskey glass in hand, and from the look in his eye, he seemed to be waiting for a performance to start. But Alex and I were like marionettes without their puppeteer. We had no idea what to do next.

"You're pretty like that," Jack said, and I saw Alex's cheeks turn pinker beneath the cotton-candy wash of blush I'd given them. "Very feminine. Although not quite female. A perfect partner for Sam, who has stepped into the masculine role tonight, without managing to look all the way like a boy."

He took a sip of his liquor and continued to stare for a moment before saying, "It's been a brutal few weeks for me, and I was looking for something different tonight. Something unusual. I don't know exactly how this idea came to mind. Maybe I took one too many drives past the windows of that sex store on Santa Monica Boulevard. Or maybe I've always wondered what Samantha would look like in the driver's seat." He was thinking aloud. That's how it seemed to me, and Alex and I remained silent, both his audience and his tiny cast.

"Kiss her, Sam," he said, and I realized he wanted me to kiss Alex, and that Alex was—for the moment—"her." I did so automatically, stepping forward, cradling Alex's face in my hands, kissing his mouth. Not able to think of him as a woman, but easily able to be turned on by the gloss of his lipstick smearing onto my own mouth.

"No, not like that," Jack sighed. "Kiss her like you like to be kissed. Kiss her the way I kiss you."

My mind whirled, but I thought I understood. I gripped the back of Alex's neck, taking charge, pulling him toward me, and I kissed him forcefully, the one in power, the one making the rules. I bit his bottom lip when we parted, and felt Alex shudder slightly at that tiny insignificant spark of pain. He towered over me in his shoes—towered even in bare feet—but still, I was the one in charge.

"Better," Jack said. "Much better."

And then we were waiting again, standing there in front of him, two actors before the director, or two naughty juveniles before the headmaster, waiting for the next command—the next direction—the next...

"Spread her out on the bed. Make her feel wanted."

Crazy stuff, this. But, of course, I didn't argue. Instead, I led Alex to the bed and he willingly lay down on his back, looking up at me. I saw trust in his eyes and that made me feel scared. He had faith in me. Faith I didn't have in myself. But when I continued to meet his gaze, I felt a bit of power transfer from Alex to myself, and I knew what to do next. If I were Jack, I'd be binding this pretty doll's wrists over her head. And so I did, without a command from my man, without a word of instruction, taking Alex's wrists and cuffing them easily, then looping the chain over the hook above our bed. Jack chuckled at this little bit of improvisation, and I could tell he approved.

I could tell Alex approved as well, because his pinafore had become a pup tent—reminding me of men I'd massaged in the past, of all the tents I'd had to avoid during my several years as a legitimate masseuse. But this was different. The tented pinafore turned me on instantly, gave me more confidence than I'd had all evening. I almost felt my own cock twitch in response. At least, it did so in my imagination.

With Alex captured so, I waited for Jack's next word,

but when I looked at him, he simply nodded. So I understood that he liked the direction I was taking. I was on my own now—for the moment—I had to be creative. And I had to be in charge.

But what did that mean exactly? I thought for a moment, considered what I most wanted to do. My eyes returned to the pup-tented pinafore, and I knew. I climbed on the bed between Alex's legs and lifted the dress. Alex's eyes were on me. Focused. I easily slid his panties down his thighs, pulling them all the way off, even over the skyscraper heels, and then I crawled back to my spot, regarding Alex's massive hard-on for only a second before dipping my head down to taste...

Chapter Thirty-Six:
Maybe Just Once

Alex groaned darkly as my mouth welcomed his cock. He arched his hips and pulled on the chains that bound his wrists, tugged with a vibrant intensity even though I knew he didn't want to get away. I licked around the tip of his cock then bobbed my head, taking more of him inside my mouth with each passing second.

Yes, I was turned on by the whole scenario, but mostly because of Jack watching. The fact that Alex was dressed as a doll didn't make me wet. It was being in charge, feeling the harness and silicone toy still in place under my jeans, and knowing precisely what I was going to be doing with them before the night was over.

Jack sipped his drink. I could feel him watching me. I could feel his eyes wandering over my body, taking in every motion. I performed for him, licking Alex, working to make his whole cock disappear down my throat. I was lost in this world, shimmying my hips, tossing my hair out of my face, until Jack's hand was on the back of my neck, gripping me like a cat grabs her kittens. Momentarily stunned, my body tensed, and I had to work to meet Jack's eyes.

"You suck cock like a girl, too," he said, an echo of our conversation out in the living room. Yet however cold his tone was, I realized he was right. I might be wearing the strap-on dick. I might be dressed—to the best of my abilities—like a boy toy, like one of those hunky men for hire out on the strip. But I was a girl. Heart and soul of a girl. Hungry mouth of a girl. Jack had my body in his strong grip, and I felt as if I wouldn't be able to breathe again until he gave permission.

"You're trying to turn me on," Jack said. "You think you're starring in some porno film, with all your hair flicking and your overacting."

He'd nailed me, yet I didn't know what he wanted, didn't know why he was chastising me.

"Like this," he said, shocking me with the rough way he pushed me aside, so that I fell back on the mattress, tripped by Alex's thigh, coming to rest on the far side of the bed. Jack gripped on to Alex's shaft, his fist firm, and he jerked the boy's cock, using my own spit as lube. Alex looked as if he were going to pass out. The mix of his current pleasure and the fear of impending pain were both vying for first place in his eyes.

Jack worked Alex with finesse. Fast and furiously, his fist pumping on Alex's cock, his face, when I dared to look up at it, intent, as if he were on a mission. There was a dangerous look in his eyes that made me quiver. I knew right then what was going to happen next. What this whole night was ultimately about. Somehow, I understood, and I felt as if the world had stopped.

No, that's not right. I felt as if my world had shattered.

But Jack managed to surprise me once more. As if he were playing his own cock, as if he were the one being jerked off, Jack seemed to nail Alex's limits to perfection. Right before the boy came, Jack glared over at me.

"Get back here."

I scrambled into position.

"Use your mouth."

I did my best. I opened my lips and sucked Alex again, this time trying to imagine I really was a boy. That Alex was my partner. That I knew all there was to know about cocks and how they worked. I sucked him harder than I had before, and Alex groaned and raised his hips, and as I felt the first shock wave of his orgasm rush through him, Jack pulled me back once more, so that Alex wet my cheeks, the edge of his pinafore, and the bed.

I wiped my face on the back of my hand and sat back on my Docs, feeling stunned. Feeling as if a movie I'd gone to see had changed midway from a comedy to a drama. Jack didn't pause for a second. He used a sheet to wipe off Alex, tossing the rumpled cotton onto the floor as he walked to the cupboard where he kept his favorite toys. I stood and moved over to the wall by the door. My heart started to race as I wondered who would be on the receiving end of Jack's wrath—wondering where his current mood had come from. He'd been easygoing out in the living room. And now, now he was a towering, frightening Dom. Alex seemed not to have sensed the change in the atmosphere, momentarily whipped by the pleasure of his climax.

Jack searched through his range of toys until he found a paddle, and I watched him grip the handle and return to the bed. I pressed back against the wall as Jack unhooked the handcuff chain, but left the cuffs in place.

"Ass in the air, now, you know the drill," was all Jack

had to say. Clearly, Alex did, rolling over on the mattress and getting onto his hands and knees. He was still in those stockings and shoes, that white dress, but now he looked like a doll after the dance, rumpled and ruined. Jack flipped the hem of the dress, revealing Alex's muscular haunches, and then he motioned to me.

I'd been watching, heart pounding, and now I was being called into duty.

"How would you spank him?" Jack asked, handing over the paddle.

I looked at Jack, looked down at Alex, and gripped the paddle. This shouldn't be difficult, right? I'd been on the other end often enough. I hesitated another moment before letting the paddle connect soundly with Alex's ass, and then again, on the other cheek, spanking steadily, firmly, until Jack stopped me. He didn't have to say the words—*you hit like a girl*—but I could hear them in my head. I thought he would demonstrate proper paddling methods, but he surprised me.

"That's not how you'd do it, kid. I know you. You're trying to please me."

I looked at him curiously, not understanding the comment. Of course I was trying to please him. Pleasing Jack was my mission. Pleasing Jack was all I understood. And now he was changing the game, changing the rules.

"How would you spank him? If you had the freedom to punish him any way you wanted. How would you do it?"

I was quiet for several seconds, and then I said to Alex, "Stand up." He moved immediately. "Bend over the bed." He obeyed as if Jack were making the requests. I lifted Alex's dress, and the movement of doing so, the drag of the fabric on his freshly shaved skin, made my pussy clench.

And I got it.

The delight in standing there, in watching Alex bend over for me, in seeing him do what I said. In watching him wait for the first blow to land. And I understood Jack's taunts—*you come like a girl, hit like a girl, lick like a girl.* He was trying to raise the power up inside of me. He was pushing me, verbally punching me, trying to get me to break out of my submissive shell, if only for a moment. If only for a night.

Never stay still. Never become stagnant.

I hefted the paddle once more, and as I did, I realized I wasn't doing this to prove something to Jack. I was doing it to prove something to myself. Which is what Jack wanted all along.

Chapter Thirty-Seven:
Free

Honestly, I didn't know why Alex was on the receiving end of this evening of punishment. I didn't know why Jack had decided to dress him in ruffles or have me do his makeup. And here's the truth: I didn't care.

I was aware only of the way the occasion made me feel. The heft of the paddle in my hand, the power behind each blow I delivered. I wasn't Dom enough to whisper any threatening words to the handsome man bent over in front of me. Even though I knew the words that would have made me the wettest had I been the one in Alex's supplicant position. Instead, I focused on the blows, striking evenly, admiring the instant rosy flush to Alex's pale skin. He had—I will say—a perfect ass. I'm not even into rear ends—why would I be, as a die-hard sub? But Alex was a fine male figure, the ideal type for an artist's model. A Michelangelo sculpture come to life.

And now, I was in charge of him. At least I was for the moment, slapping the paddle against his tender skin until

I could feel the heat of the action in my own muscles.

Alex didn't cry. I wasn't able to inflict that sort of pain, and I'd already seen him take far worse at the club under Jack's sturdy care. He didn't beg, didn't even look at me. Stoically, he took what I had to give. Almost as if he truly were a model, as if Jack were using him as a training model for me. But what would that mean?

I couldn't think about meanings now. I could only think about action.

Finally, Jack took the paddle from my hand and pushed me aside. I resumed my spot at the wall, watching as Jack undid the handcuffs and tossed them aside, then lifted Alex to standing position, removed that silly dress from him, pulled off the wig. Now, we saw Alex in the remnants of his finery—the smeared makeup, the hose and heels. He was fully hard again. My spanking had created that one response, at least. Jack could have led him around by his cock if he'd wanted. Instead, Jack said, "How do you feel?"

Alex took his time answering, completely at ease standing nearly naked in front of Jack. It was clear he didn't know what Jack wanted him to say. He weighed his words carefully, eyes focused on his boss, before trying out the word, "Fine." Simple. But would it pass?

Jack shook his head. "How do you feel about submitting to her?"

Alex wouldn't look at me. He continued to meet Jack's gaze steadily, but I saw his shoulders sag slightly. "I didn't submit to her." He seemed confused that Jack would ask this.

Jack gripped his chin in one strong hand, holding him tight. "What do you mean?"

"I submitted to you."

210

Jack smiled. His easy smile. His natural smile. It was as if Alex had won the million-dollar prize. "Good answer." It was, quite obviously, what he wanted Alex to feel. To think. It didn't matter who wielded the belt or the paddle. Didn't matter as long as the initial instruction had come from Jack.

And there I was, leaning against the wall, proud of myself for already having mastered this lesson. I'd been living with Alex as Jack's right-hand man for months now. I knew all about punishment by a second party. But there was more to Jack's night of instructions. Of course there was. Jack wouldn't be satisfied with something so simple as a post–blow job spanking. As putting Alex in his place. As showing him that there were other facets to being "more involved," as Alex had stated he wanted to be.

"Get dressed," he told Alex. "In your own clothes."

Alex kicked off the heels immediately and pulled off the hose. Then he stood unconsciously, so beautifully naked, and dressed once more. He looked different now. Even in his slightly rumpled preppy gear. With the makeup still on, he had that rock star edge, and I found him actually sexy—something I hadn't really considered before. Up until now, he had simply been an extension of Jack.

Jack motioned for me, and I hurried to his side, ready to be sent into battle. Ready to be cast onstage. "And you?" he said, running his hands along my shoulders and down my sides. "What are you thinking about?"

He didn't only want to dominate my body. Jack wanted to rule my mind.

I shook my head. I felt as if I were spinning. I didn't know what to think.

"We're not done. You know that."

I nodded. "Yes, Jack."

"So what might I have planned for you next?"

I looked over at Alex, waiting by my vanity, his kohl-rimmed eyes and tousled hair almost deviantly erotic. I had an idea. But I didn't speak right away. Jack knew I was holding back, and his hand came up, quickly, slapping my cheek, bringing me into focus once more. My own hand went up instantly, rubbing away the sting, and I managed to whisper, "You're going to have me fuck him."

Jack laughed, dark and low. "No, kid. I'm going to have you fuck each other. But now, you're on a more even playing field." His hand slid down farther to press against the cock in my jeans. "Now, you've got a fighting chance to get on top..."

Chapter Thirty-Eight:
What Now?

A fighting chance.

What did that mean exactly? Were Alex and I supposed to engage in some sort of Greco-Roman combat for Jack's viewing pleasure, rolling around on the destroyed white sheets in an erotic attempt to get on top? Had I been correct in envisioning Jack as some sort of Caesar? Twisted. Wicked. Power drunk.

I stared at him, waiting for further instructions while my mind raced ahead. What had I thought tonight would be about? Alex simply taking it up the ass? Willingly? Like a humble servant? Sure, he bowed down to Jack's rule in all visible manners. But there was nothing in his personality that should have made me think he would bend over and spread 'em at my command.

And who was I to give commands anyway?

I wondered if Alex was thinking similar thoughts. He didn't appear nearly as nervous as I felt. Rather, Jack's words had given him at least a momentary sense of calm.

Maybe he'd been worried all evening, and now he was finally able to relax. I don't know. I'm not Alex.

Jack looked at me and said, "First, you need to start with an even playing field."

"What do you mean?"

"What do you think?"

I hated questions like this. Because if I said something wrong, I might give Jack a more filthy idea than he'd already had. But with his eyes on me, so telling, I said, "You're going to spank me."

"Really? That's what you think?"

I looked at the floor. "Alex is."

"Give the girl a prize," Jack murmured. Then, to his boy, "How do you want her?"

"Stripped down."

There was no use in arguing. Any pleasure I had won from spanking Alex was now a distant memory. While the men watched, I undid my Docs and kicked them off. I pulled off my shirt and sports bras until I stood as naked as Alex had been, except for that harness sporting my vibrant blue erection. I felt a little silly, actually. If I had known I was going to be on top, I would have been able to slide into that attitude. But Jack's words echoed in my head: I had a fighting chance. I would much rather have been forced into submission, led to the bed and cuffed, given no opportunity to fight at all. That scenario was far more my speed. But here I was, nervously eyeing Alex, waiting for Jack's next instruction.

The words didn't come from Jack.

"Bend over. Touch your toes."

I could do this. I've always been flexible. But Alex must have known it was my least favorite way to get a spanking. I'd have preferred being spread on the bed. Or pulled over his lap. Or bent over a chair. This way meant I had to work on staying balanced. I didn't bother to watch as he chose his implement of pain. I shut my eyes and waited for the spanking to begin.

But Alex was in a mood. He took his time. This was payback, and he relished every fucking second.

"Straighten your legs," Alex said, and I obeyed, knowing I'd never get it right for him. He wanted something beyond perfection. He wanted to show Jack what a good Dom he could be. "Prepare yourself," he said, and I heard the laughter in his voice. There was no way to do this, and he knew it. No way to get ready for that first, startling blow.

He spanked me hard, pressing one hand into my lower back to make me arch my ass even higher, forcing me onto my tiptoes, but using the weight of his palm to keep me steady. He slammed the paddle into me, and I worked to keep from crying out. He didn't make me count, which I was grateful for in one way, but fearful of in another. Not having to count meant there was no foreseeable end in sight. Alex was going to spank me until...well, until he was done. (Like that line a military friend told me about—his commander saying, "You'll do those push-ups until *I* get tired.")

I felt tears in my eyes and hated myself for them. I hadn't made Alex cry. But there I was, being a girl all over again, humiliated and humbled, on display for both of the men. I wished I hadn't bought this type of harness, the one with the fully exposed back. It gave Alex the perfect frame of my ass to cover with blow after blow, until Jack gripped his hand and pulled him away.

"She's done," he said. "For the moment, at least."

I sighed and stood up, not giving Alex the pleasure of

seeing me rub my heated cheeks, but shooting him a look of pure venom, nonetheless. While I stood there, waiting, Jack undressed Alex once more. He seemed to enjoy this part of the evening, giving us power and then taking it away. Alex appeared less confident once he was naked again.

"You'll need lube," Jack said next. "Both of you."

I felt dizzy as he poured a handful of the clear liquid into my palm. I'd already been chastised for not jerking my cock the way a real man would, and now Jack wanted me to lube myself up. There was no way I could do this convincingly. I watched Alex, fisting his cock, getting obvious and instant pleasure at the sensation of flesh on flesh. I was at a disadvantage, wasn't I? My cock was plastic. But if I pressed down right, the base hit my clit, winning me a spark of sweetness.

"On the bed," Jack said next, not giving me any time to worry now. Taking full charge as the director of this X-rated romp. "Sam, I want you on your back."

Alex smirked at me, and it seemed I'd lost before the games had begun. On my back, with my legs over Alex's shoulders, his cock ready as Jack said, "Now, fuck her." He was about to, his body poised, when Jack pulled him back, physically pushing Alex off me.

"You'd let him, wouldn't you?"

My eyes widened.

"You'd let him slide inside you. You wouldn't balk at all."

"But—"

"But what?"

"You told him, you told me—" I was stammering, making no sense. But Jack wasn't making any sense either, was he?

"I said you had a fighting chance," Jack repeated, and then I got it. He didn't want to choreograph the whole event. He wanted to see what we would do if left to our own devices. I had felt empty, waiting for the Master to input information. When I looked into Jack's eyes, I saw what he wanted. More than a show with him as the writer. He wanted live action, that wrestling match I'd imagined. A fighting chance. He'd said it, and he meant it. I looked over at Alex, and I saw that his confidence level seemed to have slipped a bit. He was staring at Jack in awe.

"Let's try that again," Jack said, stepping back, and I felt that wave of power come over me once more. Jack was giving me permission. And I could do with that freedom what I would.

Alex climbed onto the bed, looking wary. There was no way I could beat him with strength. No way at all. I had to be wily. Clever. I had to be a girl.

He didn't speak to me. He sat back on his knees, staring, waiting, until I came forward and pressed my body to his. I cradled his face in my hands. I kissed him. Softly. Kissed his cheeks and his lips and when he closed his eyes, kissed his eyelids. I stroked my fingers through his hair, let my fingertips trail down the muscles of his arms. Alex shivered, put off balance by the candy of my caress.

Yes, I had a cock between my legs. But I was a girl.

I let my lips trail down the hollow of his throat. I kissed his chest, and worked my way along his flat belly. I pushed him back on the bed, gripping his hard-on in one hand while I continued to trick my lips along the tender skin of his inner thighs.

Alex groaned and arched his hips. I heard Jack chuckle behind me. He seemed to understand what I was doing, seemed to guess my plan. But he didn't say a word. He simply watched.

Slowly, sensuously, I worked my way back up Alex's strong body. I didn't let him feel the cock against him. I teased him, pinching his nipples, then lifting his arms over his head and licking along the lines of his muscles. Moving from one bicep to the other. Carefully making my way to his wrists. I had reached for the cuffs, discarded after our previous encounter, but Alex opened his eyes before I could get one on.

"What the fuck—?" He was in motion instantly, on me, grabbing the cuffs from my hand as he tussled with me on the bed. I'd hoped to at least manage to get one cuff on before he rebelled, but that didn't seem possible now. Alex easily pinned me down, and in seconds the cuffs were on my own wrists, and Jack was laughing once more.

"Good try," he said, coming closer to the bed. Alex wasn't moving. I felt his weight on top of me, keeping me in place. My wrists were cuffed, but he hadn't fastened the chain to the hook. "You wanted to lull him into trusting you."

My breath was coming rapid now. I felt like a trapped animal. But I wasn't scared in the slightest.

"So let's see how you get yourself out of this one," whispered Jack. "Let's see…."

Looking back now, it all seems so damn debauched. Jack, the ringmaster. And the two of us, willing subjects, off-centered players. Who were we? This trio of misfits in the bedroom of a penthouse over Sunset? What tied us together aside from our twisted fantasies? And yet—I always have to compare things to life with Byron—how was this any darker than what I'd already lived through? No, my ex never raised a hand to me, but I'd been put

down in a cage for so many years, lived without light.
This world seemed heavenly to me.

Freedom like I'd never even imagined.

Chapter Thirty-Nine:
What Would You Do?

I'm not a magician. I'm no Houdini—or even a modern, female version of Houdini. I was cuffed, and Alex outweighed me by seventy pounds, and I was pinned down on the bed.

Where do we go now?

Where indeed?

Jack seemed amused by the whole situation. Pleased, in fact, by the way I'd handled myself up to this point, and the ultimate indignity of having the cuffs that I'd tried to put on Alex wind up on my own wrists.

But when I looked into Alex's eyes, I wasn't scared. I saw something there. Saw—not fear. Not hesitation or nervousness...but kindness. I had to call it that in my mind, searching still for a better description. This was an emotion I rarely saw when staring at Alex. Generally, Alex was performing some task for Jack, and he had the give and take of a robot. But now, he actually seemed to feel for me. I stared back at him, and then realized, that no, he wasn't looking at me kindly, he was looking at me with pity. And that changed everything.

I would not have him feel sorry for me. No way. Sure, my wrists were cuffed, and sure, he was superior physically, but I would not roll over and give in. I would not do what I'd imagined from him—bending and spreading—at a word, at a nod.

The atmosphere seemed to shift in the room for me, changing in seconds as I backed up against the wall behind the bed, my cuffed wrists in front of me, wary, waiting.

Alex tilted his head at me, and he seemed now to sense danger. "You're not thinking of fighting."

A statement, not a question. Besides, it came from Alex, not Jack. I didn't have to say a word to him. Not a fucking word.

How long was this night going on, anyway? Felt like years since I'd first dressed the boy. And now, look at us. Fighters on a mattress ring. Circling, at least, with our eyes.

"Tell me you're not, Sam."

"If I did, I'd be lying."

He looked at me again with those pity-filled eyes, and I wanted to scratch him.

"It's too easy with you bound like that. All I have to do is grab you, flip you over, and I'm in you—one, two, three."

"Then take the cuffs off."

"Why would I do that?"

I kept him talking, sizing up the situation as I did. It wasn't that I didn't feel aroused. Let me make that clear. I was turned on beyond belief. Knowing Jack was watching was one thing. But Alex and I were like two characters on a sitcom who hate each other on the surface, but deep

221

down trade erotic sparks. We were probably destined to fuck at some point. Why not tonight?

"Why would I take off the cuffs?" Alex asked again. He turned then, to look at Jack, perhaps to see what his boss thought of all this, and that was all I needed. I pushed him, not hard, but firmly—my bare foot in his chest, knocking him off balance enough to get around him on the bed. I didn't have any plans. Didn't have any idea at all. But I was out of the room in a hurry, that ridiculous cock still harnessed to my body, trying to figure out my next move.

No, I wasn't going to sprint out of the apartment. I only wanted to get to some private corner where I could clear my mind. It didn't matter if ultimately I was brought back to the bedroom and fucked senseless. I knew, based on the constant, heady pulse from my clit that I reveled in the thought.

But Jack had said: a fighting chance. I wasn't going down without a struggle.

Alex was behind me in seconds, but I'd made it to the kitchen, pressed my back against the fridge, hands still cuffed in front of me. He didn't appear angry at all. The action was thrilling to him. Nothing easy about this evening. Nothing sane.

"Why, Sam?" he said again, but softer this time, as he came forward, pressing his own body up against mine. "Why would I uncuff you, when it's so much more fun to take you like this." In a flash, he'd gripped the chain of the cuffs and pulled it upward, making me rise up to my tiptoes. He dragged me a few steps to the left, spinning me around to face the cabinets, and he hooked the chain onto the knob of one of the cabinets, forcing me to stay on my tiptoes, fully stretched. I couldn't pull the chain off the knobs. I couldn't spin around to face Alex because his body was flat against mine, pinning me to the counter.

"Answer me," he said.

I was breathless, the harness now digging into me, the synthetic cock pressed flat and up against my body.

"I don't know," I said, my voice as soft as his. "I don't know, Alex."

His hands slid down my naked body, coming to rest on the cheeks of my ass. Very slowly, he spread them apart, and I lowered my head, waiting.

"That's it?" His mouth to my neck. "That's all you got, tough guy?"

I'd thought I'd been pretty clever, actually. Getting this far. But now, he was taunting me. The winner, getting ready to claim his prize. Yet I was trapped.

What did he want me to do?

Alex reached into a nearby cabinet and pulled out a bottle of imported olive oil. Jack and I rarely ever cooked. But we did have the most expensive ingredients around. Just in case one of us felt like playing house. Alex poured a river of this organic lube between my rear cheeks and then rested the head of his cock against me, waiting. I don't know who he thought I was or what he thought I was capable of doing. I couldn't vanish. I couldn't do a thing.

"Really?" he murmured again. "That's all the fight in you?"

And then I had an idea. Turning my head slightly, I said, "Is it me you really want to fuck?"

He hesitated.

"I mean, isn't it Jack you want to bend over? Or is it Jack you want to bend over for? Why are you on me, Alex? Why aren't oiling up your dick and showing it off to him."

He'd frozen behind me. I was fighting with the thing I knew best: with words.

"Or is that what you guys did before we met? Is that the secret nobody is willing to share with me? The elephant in the room that neither of you will talk about. When you had your little foursomes, did you two ever cross swords?"

He was still behind me, absolutely still. I took over then, pressing back the slightest bit, pushing myself against his rock-hard cock. My body shuddered at the immediate pleasure of that delicious sensation.

"Is that what this is all about?" I asked next. "A way to reveal secrets to me...?" Again I pressed back lightly, and now Alex moaned, making me feel a tiny bit more powerful. How bizarre. Standing naked and cuffed in the kitchen, yet my words giving me the spark of power I craved. At least, until Jack joined the party.

"Would it change things?" I turned my head quickly to the doorway. There was Jack. He took a step forward, and then pushed Alex away from me. Then it was Jack behind me, pressing his body to mine. Jack fully dressed, not giving a damn about ruining his expensive slacks with the spreading stain of olive oil.

Would it? Jack pressed firmly against me, letting me feel how hard he was. I squeezed my eyes closed, not knowing what to do. What to say.

"Tell me, Samantha."

He turned my head sideways, tilted my chin, forced me to meet his eyes.

"Tell me."

Chapter Forty:
A Kind of Magic

Magic is all about secrets. The hidden slit in a coat pocket. The unnoticed compartment in a black silk top hat. But relationships should be about truth and honesty. There should be no secrets between lovers, right?

Jack wanted my answer before he told me the question. He wanted me to absolve him, to release him, to relax him before he explained the truth. Before he revealed the man—or was it men?—who were hidden behind the curtain.

And yet, there he was, his cock against me, shielded by his Italian slacks. Fulfilling one more of my most treasured kinks. I adore being naked with a lover who is still clothed. I like that off-balance sensation. I know my hot buttons well by now. My purest fantasy? The one that gets me off every time? Odd, I think, for a sub to have it, but Jack understood that one right away. Having a man take my place, or rather, having a lover take the pain for me. Not to say that I can't withstand it myself. But what Jack did in that New York club, shielding my body with his... thinking of it now makes me almost turn to cream.

But back to Jack. He wanted me to say that nothing mattered. That he could confess anything to me, tell me that he'd been shooting up and it wouldn't have changed my feelings. That he'd been selling drugs on the street corner, or hooking up with the pretty boys on Sunset, or spending all of his money on the ponies, and I'd still gaze up with my adoring eyes and say, "Doesn't change a thing."

And you know what? I've been there. With Brock, the vices didn't color my view of him. The drugs, the stolen bikes, the scars from fights, the off-hour phone calls for bail. None of that made me flee. If anything, I was addicted to the electricity of the vices. Craved the excitement of his world. Found "normal" life difficult afterward. So bland. So fucking boring. How did average people exist without the drama?

But Jack wasn't asking me to accept him with all of his flaws. He was asking me... Jesus, I didn't even know for sure what he was asking me.

"Tell me, Sam."

"You tell me," I countered, buying time again, aware I had little bargaining chips in this situation. Cuffed as I was and mounted on the cabinet, there was nowhere for me to go. No place to run or hide. But I was also aware that Jack had now entered the action. He wasn't the sole member of the audience anymore. He was an active player.

"If the things you said were true, what would that mean for you?"

I hated like hell to be right. What would it mean? What would it mean to me if Jack and Alex were lovers as well as boss and employee? What would it mean if Jack fucked Alex the way that he fucked me? Before I could answer those questions, new ones rose up, exploding like fireworks in my mind...what would it mean if Jack touched Alex the way he touched me, gently stroking his face, kissing his open mouth. What would it mean if he pressed up against Alex and told him that he loved him?

That's when the tears started.

Because Alex wasn't a vice, like playing the ponies or drinking too much whiskey.

Alex was a competitor.

Jack had promised me no other women, back in the club, after that night when I'd been held up in the puppy cage. And Alex's name had come up, but we hadn't focused on it. Hadn't gone there. What should I have asked for on that night? Exclusivity? What did I really want?

That was simple. I wanted to be Jack's alone. I wanted to be his one and only.

And now, somehow, even while feeling Jack's strong body behind mine, I could sense Alex watching from mere feet away. Now, I knew that I wasn't.

As I say endlessly, I have always thought of myself as monogamous (despite my tendency to stray). It's a strange statement, I know. My feelings hadn't changed in spite of the fact that I regularly let my lover's assistant have his way with me—in any way he'd been instructed by Jack. I didn't consider us to be in a three-way relationship. Didn't think that I was part of a polyamorous threesome.

Was that what Jack wanted?

Was that why Alex was so put out?

I'd taken his place. I'd usurped his position.

"Tell me," Jack demanded, and I lowered my head to my chest, feeling the strain in my arms, feeling as if I might cry for days and never stop. I wanted Jack the way

I wanted air. That is to say, I didn't really want him. I needed him. Craved him. No, I hadn't gotten the piercings he'd requested, but I wouldn't have balked for a second had he led me to a tattoo parlor instead and asked me to submit to being adorned with a '40s-style heart with a banner bearing his name. And now he was asking me how I'd feel if I had to share him. Or rather he was telling me that I'd been sharing him all along. Was that right? Had I made the correct assumptions based on the evening's events?

Jack's hands were on me, sliding up and down my arms. I knew how turned on I was, knew that if he unzipped his trousers and pushed into me, he would find me more than wet, more than mildly aroused. There was a sea of liquid sex between my legs.

But first Jack wanted my answer. And I couldn't say the words.

"You've known," he whispered next. "You have to have known. Alex's been with me for years. We're not..." he hesitated, rare for Jack, who always seemed to have the right words to say. "We're not exactly lovers." I knew he was being cautious because Alex was standing right there. "Not exactly. But..."

"But you have been," I guessed, and Jack said, "Yes."

My mind raced. They'd been together. But they were not always together. Alex loved Jack, but...but...Jack didn't love Alex. Not the same way he loved me. Was that what he was telling me?

"Can you deal with that? Can you live with that?"

I looked over at Alex, who still seemed amazingly at ease being naked, his eyeliner now fully smeared, the lipstick on his full lips all but gone, a rosy shadow all that remained. He was absolutely and crushingly handsome, and he was waiting as submissively as he possibly could. Not getting involved in the discussion. Not butting in.

Could I live with what Jack was describing—or what I thought he was describing? Could I accept that Jack would never solely be mine?

It wasn't even a question.

I said, "Yes," and Jack moved quickly, lifting up the handcuff chain and gripping me in his arms. He carried me back to the bedroom, Alex following. He spread me down on the bed, the way I'd imagined earlier in the evening. The way I like best. No need to think, or plan, or fight. Spread me out and looked down on me, as if I were some glittering prize he'd won at a carnival, showing off his strength.

Alex slid on his slacks without his boxers and watched as Jack fucked me. Sweetly fucked me, still in his clothes, his pants on but open. Fucked me until I came, shaking the bed with the power of my climax. Lost in the fact that I lived in an imperfect world, with a man who knew me so perfectly. Lost in the fact that dreams do come true, oh yes, they do, but you might have to share the stage with someone else's dreams, as well.

"Tell me," Jack whispered as he stroked my body afterward. "Tell me."

"I love you, Jack."

His eyes seemed to glaze for a moment. Shimmer within. And when he looked at me—there it was—magic.

About the Author

Called "a trollop with a laptop" by *East Bay Express,* "a literary siren" by Good Vibrations, and "the mistress of literary erotica" by Violet Blue, Alison Tyler is naughty and she knows it.

Over the past two decades, Ms. Tyler has written more than twenty-five explicit novels, including *Tiffany Twisted, Melt with You, The ESP Affair,* and *Dark Secret Love: A Story of Submission,* the volume that precedes *The Delicious Torment* in a trilogy. Her novels and short stories have been translated into Japanese, Dutch, German, Italian, Norwegian, Spanish and Greek. When not writing sultry short stories, she edits erotic anthologies, including *Alison's Wonderland, Naughty Fairy Tales from A to Z, Kiss My Ass, Cuffed,* and *Playing with Fire.* She is also the author of several novellas including *Cuffing Kate, Giving In, A Taste of Chi,* and *Those Girls.*

Ms. Tyler is loyal to coffee (black), lipstick (red), and tequila (straight). She has tattoos, but no piercings; a wicked tongue, but a quick smile; and bittersweet memories, but no regrets. She believes it won't rain if she doesn't bring an umbrella, prefers hot and dry to cold and wet, and loves to spout her favorite motto: *You can sleep when you're dead*. She chooses Led Zeppelin over the Beatles, the Cure over NIN, and the Stones over everyone. Yet although she appreciates good rock, she has a pitiful weakness for eighties hair bands.

In all things important, she remains faithful to her partner of eighteen years, but she still can't choose just one perfume.